A DATING COACH MYSTERY

JOAN DONALDSON-YARMEY

Renaissance.
Diverse Canadian Voices

First edition, 2024

Cover art and design by Nathan Fréchette. Typesetting by Nathan Fréchette. Edited by Molly Desson and Myryam Ladouceur. Proofreading by Deanna Broodhagen.

Legal deposit, Library and Archives Canada, May 2024.

Paperback ISBN: 978-1-990086-70-0
Ebook ISBN: 978-1-990086-76-2
Renaissance Press - pressesrenaissancepress.ca

Renaissance acknowledges that it is hosted on the traditional, unceded land of the Anishinabek, the Kanien'kehá:ka, and the Omàmìwininìwag. We acknowledge the privileges and comforts that colonialism has granted us and vow to use this privilege to disrupt colonialism by lifting up the voices of marginalized humans who continue to suffer the ongoing effects of ongoing colonialism.

Printed in Gatineau by:

Imprimerie Gauvin - Depuis 1892 - gauvin.ca

To Matthew Anthony Yarmey
September 26, 1970 - February 17, 2024

You slipped quietly away
In the middle of the night
You took us all by surprise
By going to the light.

We didn't get a chance to say
Our last fond farewell
To wish you a safe journey.
Our tears we cannot quell.

CHAPTER 1

Jenna Hamilton and Adam Olsen entered the Vancouver Convention Centre, and looked for the sign that would point them to Carla Bell and Bruce Everett's engagement party. They spied the poster and followed the arrow to the East Ballroom C. The door was propped open and laughter and conversation drifted towards them as they approached.

Adam smiled, as he waited for Jenna to enter first. "Sounds like the party is in full swing."

Jenna stepped into the large room full of guests dressed in evening clothes. Streamers were strung on the ceiling and draped down the walls. A large sign with the words 'Congratulations Carla and Bruce' hung above a long, decorated table to the left. To the right was a stage with the instruments set up by the band that would later play during the dance. In between, men and women mingled amongst round tables, champagne flutes in their hands.

"Good evening," said a man standing just inside the door. He wore a white shirt, black pants, and black bowtie. "My name is Richard and I am here to assist you with anything you need."

Jenna smiled at him as a woman came over with a tray of glasses. She and Adam each took one.

"I don't see Carla or Bruce," Jenna said, scanning the crowd. "Do you?"

Adam looked over the heads of the throng. "Nope, don't see them." He was tall and could almost be called skinny. His straight, brown hair fell into his eyes and Jenna knew he sometimes trimmed it himself. He was handsome in his grey suit, blue shirt, and darker blue.

"Probably going to make a dramatic entrance," Jenna said, as she took a sip of champagne. She'd known Carla Bell for years, having worked for her in the early days of her starting the Alcove Printing Company. They had remained friends after Jenna left to open a bookstore with Adam. Carla was in her forties and the company now had franchises nationwide. She was a very rich woman.

"Look for Hillary and Drake. Hillary said they might be a little late."

"I don't see them either."

A voice vibrated through the room, "Excuse me! Excuse me!"

As everyone turned to the stage, Jenna recognized Carla's younger sister, Monica, holding a microphone as she waited for the conversation to stop. She was in a mauve dress, her hair piled in curls on her head. Jenna marvelled at how much she resembled Carla.

"Thank you all for coming," Monica said, once the room was quiet. She surveyed the crowd. "You all know why we're here, so without further ado, I'd like to present the bride- and groom-to-be, Carla and Bruce!"

Monica swept her arm towards the right wing of the stage. There was a pause, and then Carla and Bruce walked on stage holding hands. Bruce was in a black suit with a magenta shirt and black tie, while Carla wore a bright magenta floral-print dress that reached just above her ankles. She had a matching flower in her blonde hair, which she wore in a long bob with bangs. Jenna had never seen her look so beautiful, or so happy.

While everyone clapped and whistled for the couple, Monica wrapped her arms around Carla and handed her the microphone before hugging Bruce and slipping off the stage.

2

Carla and Bruce stood with an arm around each other's waist while they waited for the cheering to quiet down.

"Bruce and I are so happy that you could all join us for this exciting evening. There's an open bar and Richard at the door will be happy to call you a taxi if you want one. The meal will be served shortly and then after a few short speeches, the dancing will begin! So drink up, eat up, and enjoy this celebration of our love."

Again, the crowd erupted with applause and yelling. Carla handed the microphone to Bruce who beamed out at everyone. Eventually, the din settled enough that he was able to say a few words.

"This is the second-best day of my life; the best one is yet to come, when we actually tie the knot. I just want to echo Carla's words and invite you to take pleasure in our love and happiness this evening which is just a prelude to the partying that will take place on our actual wedding day."

For the third time, the room resonated with the cheers of the happy crowd.

Jenna finished her champagne just as she was approached by a man carrying a tray of fresh drinks. She exchanged her empty glass for a full one as Adam did the same. It had been a long time since she or Adam had been in a party mood. Last week, she'd bought an above-the-knee black dress with a curved neckline and long, flowing sleeves for the occasion. Today, she had gone to Hillary's Salon and Spa, which was just down from their bookstore in the Net Loft, for a manicure and to have her natural curly hair styled. In heels, she reached just above Adam's shoulders.

"Shall we find our table?" Adam asked, as much of the crowd began sitting.

They wandered through the round tables that were covered with lilac-coloured tablecloths, the centre of each holding a large bouquet of flowers surrounded by tea lights in glass holders. They found their gold-printed white place cards and sat. Jenna placed her champagne flute beside an already filled glass of water and draped her purse strap and her black shawl over the back of the chair. Adam continued to sip on his champagne.

Jenna was happy to see that two of their fellow tablemates were women she'd worked with at Carla's company. She nodded to Sadie and Patricia and introduced Adam as her business partner, and they, in turn, were presented to their husbands. The other two places were empty. The three couples chatted a bit, with Jenna catching up on what Sadie and Patricia had been doing since she'd last seen them.

"We made it," Hillary said, breathlessly.

Jenna smiled at Hillary Greenwood and Dr. Drake Ferrell. Hillary was tall and slender with a head of thick, shoulder-length hair. Last spring, Hillary had been in a car that had been involved in an accident and the driver, her employee Bruno, had died. Jenna and Adam had solved the mystery of who Bruno really was and why someone had deliberately killed him. Hillary and Carla had become friends through Jenna and, besides doing Jenna's hair for the evening, Hillary had also styled Carla's.

Years ago, before he'd become a doctor, Jenna had been in a relationship with Drake. It had lasted almost three years but ended a year after Drake's nephew had been killed. They'd remained friends, though, occasionally having dinner together, calling each other on birthdays and holidays, and being there when one of them needed someone to talk to. Jenna still cared for

4

the handsome man and had been happy when he and Hillary had begun dating after the accident.

Jenna introduced Hillary and Drake to their table companions and there was sporadic conversation as the last of the crowd found their tables. When everyone was seated, Carla and Bruce entered from a room off the side of the stage followed by an entourage of three other couples. The only one Jenna recognized was Monica. The other two women wore mauve dresses that matched hers. The men were dressed in black suits and magenta shirts like Bruce.

The crowd clapped as they walked across the room to the head table with a lilac tablecloth and black napkins. Vases of flowers ran its length, large candles in hurricane holders in between. Carla and Bruce stopped behind the two centre chairs while the women continued past to stand on Carla's right and the men stayed on Bruce's left.

The entourage waited until Carla and Bruce were seated then sat themselves. Immediately, the catering staff, dressed in black slacks and white shirts or blouses, emerged from a door at the back of the room with large trays full of bowls of salad. Two went to the head table and set bowls in front of Clara and Bruce and their party while the rest started with the guest tables. When their trays were empty, the servers hurried away for more. Everyone had a salad in front of them in less than two minutes.

Jenna was impressed with their efficiency and happy that the dressing on the salad was Thousand Island, her favourite. There was little conversation as everyone ate. The servers seemed to have a schedule, because Jenna had barely finished eating when her bowl was whisked away along with everyone else's and a new round of trays came out with the main course. When Jenna had received the invitation to the engagement party, she had been asked to select what type of meal she and her guest preferred: regular or gluten free roast beef and chicken meals and vegan shepherd's pie. The plates, chicken for both of them, were set in front of them without anything being said.

For dessert, plates with a variety of cakes, cookies, and squares were placed on the tables. There was laughter as the plates were passed around so everyone could check out what was on them and then choose what they wanted. There wasn't enough of one type for each person to sample but there were enough so they could try two or three different ones. Jenna took a bar with some sort of crumble topping and one that looked like it had candies on top. Adam picked a chocolate chip cookie and a square with a swirl of icing.

"I'm not much on sweets," Drake said. He looked over the array and finally selected a peanut butter/mallow bar.

"I have to watch my waistline," Hillary said and only took a cream puff with caramel drizzled over it. When everyone had picked something, they compared tastes as they tried them.

"My crumble tastes like it's got strawberry and lemon in it," Jenna said. She turned the morsel over in her mouth. "Not that bad of a combination."

"It looks like this cookie has a piece of brownie in it," Adam said, showing it around the table.

"How does it taste?" Drake asked.

"Chocolatey, very chocolatey."

They discussed Drake's peanut butter/marshmallow bar, which he said had a lot of peanut butter in it, and Hillary's cream puff with caramel drizzle. 'Delicious' was her comment. The other couples also liked the cheesecake with raspberry swirls and the mini key lime pies. Coffee was served, the plates were cleared away, and the staff with the champagne trays began circulating again.

"I think I'll go to the bar and get a beer." Adam stood. "Anyone want anything?"

"No, thank you," the others said.

Drake joined him. "I'll come with you."

Jenna watched the two men walk away. She and Adam had known each other since they'd shared an English class at university. Adam had specialized in business management, while Jenna had received a degree in sociology as well as one in English language and literature. While they were in university, they'd discovered that they both wanted to own a bookstore. It had taken them five years after graduation to finally make it happen, both of them working and saving their money until they had a down payment. It had taken another year of searching to find the right bookstore for sale.

They'd now owned A Novel Bookshop—one of the few remaining independent bookstores in Vancouver—for almost four years. They were situated on the ground floor of the two-storey Net Loft on Granville Island and sold both new and used books. Last year, they'd branched out to include magazines, knick-knacks like dragons and unicorns to go with fantasy books, and novelties such as jewellery boxes, decorative napkins, and ornaments. They ordered most of their books from distributers representing publishing houses but also had a small section for self-published books. For their used-book section, they either bought them outright or the customer was able to pick one book for every two they brought in. While they weren't getting rich, they were getting by and both were happy with their decision.

Neither she nor Adam had had much success in the dating game, even though she was a dating coach. Their success seemed to be in solving mysteries. Jenna had been glad when Adam agreed to be her plus one for this engagement party. She disliked attending affairs like this alone.

Adam and Drake, each with a beer, came back to the table just as the speeches were beginning. First Monica stood, microphone in hand. "Hi. In case anyone doesn't know who I am, I am lucky enough to be Carla's younger sister, Monica. The woman to my right is our cousin, Lillian, and beside her is Carla's best friend, Rachael."

She waited until the applause subsided. "I want to say how happy I am that my sister is getting married to the most amazing man, Bruce. He is kind, sweet, and generous and has fit into our family perfectly."

The crowd clapped and Bruce raised his glass to her. She smiled back.

"That's all I am going to say now. I will save the rest for their wedding day, but while I have your attention, I want to ask all of you for your help. As some of you know, I just got engaged last month."

She paused as there was a smattering of applause.

"Thank you. My groom-to-be, Kevin, is out there somewhere in the audience. Kevin, would you please stand."

Jenna craned her neck and finally spotted a young man with a receding hairline standing at one of the tables. He shyly waved a hand then sat down.

"Thank you, Kevin," Monica smiled. "So what I want help with is for all of you to harass my sister and Bruce into agreeing to have a double wedding with Kevin and me."

There was a lot of hooting and hollering as the crowd seemed to agree with Monica. She turned, grinned at Carla, and pointed to the gathering. "See, they want us to do the double wedding."

Carla shook her finger at Monica then looked at Bruce who gave a slight nod. With a smile, Carla stood and leaned into the microphone. "She's been after us ever since Bruce and I announced our engagement. We've discussed it and I guess by popular demand... we agree to have a double wedding with Monica and Kevin!"

The racket increased with the addition of whistling. Monica threw her arms around Carla's neck and the two hugged. When Carla sat down again, Monica turned back to the audience.

"Thank you, everyone. My greatest wish has come true. And since Kevin and I were the ones who wanted the double wedding, we will leave the setting and the date up to Carla and Bruce."

She sat down among the clamour and passed the microphone to Carla, who then handed it to Bruce, who gave it to the man on his left. The man stood and waited for the room to be silent.

"Most of you don't know me, but I am Ronnie, one-third of the Bruce, Ronnie, and Bill trio. The handsome man to my left is Bill, and next to him is Mason, Bruce's cousin."

When the clapping subsided, Ronnie continued, "Bruce, Bill, and I have been in each other's lives since we were all five years old, and I'm happy to announce that, after all these years, Bruce and I have decided to go into business together. I'm proud to be here with him now as he celebrates his engagement to the most wonderful woman. But like Monica, I'll save the juicy stories for the wedding."

People's hands must be getting sore, Jenna thought as there was another round of applause.

Carla and Bruce stood together as Bruce took the microphone from Ronnie. "As we said earlier we're so happy that you could join us for our engagement party. We'll let you know when the wedding is but for now, the band will soon start playing so enjoy the next phase of our party."

The band tuned their instruments as the guests wandered around greeting people they knew. Little groups formed as they chatted.

"I'm going to get some pictures of Carla and her hairstyle," Hillary said. "It's about time I had a new poster of one of my satisfied customers up on my wall. Plus, I can post it on my Instagram as well."

Hillary, with Drake following, worked her way through the crowd to the head table. Jenna and Adam remained at their table. Other than their fellow tablemates, neither of them knew any of the other guests.

"Are you a friend of Dorothy's?"

Jenna turned to see Mason looking down at Adam.

"Why, yes I am," Adam smiled up at him. "A good friend."

"Would you like a drink?"

"Another beer would be great." Adam stood and they walked away together.

Who's Dorothy? Jenna wondered. She'd known Adam a long time, and he had never mentioned a friend or relative named Dorothy. She'd have to ask why he'd kept her a secret later. She watched as Adam and Mason looked like they were exchanging phone numbers on their cell phones at the bar then clinked their beers before drinking.

The band started playing a waltz. Mason put his bottle back on the bar and hurried over to Rachael. They lined up with the rest of

10

the entourage behind Carla and Bruce, and the four couples swept onto the dance floor. The guests stood in a circle watching them. Jenna was curious about what their wedding was going to be like, since their engagement party seemed to be following the conventions of a wedding reception.

"Come join us," Carla beckoned the crowd. "Come on."

A few couples merged with the group on the floor and when the waltz finished, the band switched to a faster two-step. Carla and Bruce left the floor while others stepped onto it. The music changed constantly from slow to fast. Some were for couples to dance together and others, like "The Twist", were for distance dancing. Hillary and Drake spent most of their time on the dance floor. Jenna remembered how much Drake liked to dance. They'd even taken ball room dance lessons together before their split.

Jenna was content to sit and watch with Adam. They were comfortable in each other's company. Jenna thought of asking about Dorothy but decided she didn't want to yell over the music.

When the band took a short break and the other couples came back to the table, everyone made small talk about how good the band was and how much fun they were having. The first song after the band's break was the "Chicken Dance" and Jenna persuaded Adam to get up with her. They laughed as they clucked and clapped their hands, flapped their arms, and wiggled their butts along with the rest of the dancers.

When that was over, the band switched to a country song and guests lined up for a line dance. Jenna had been taking line dancing classes for the past couple of months and she stood on the edge of the dance floor to see what dance they would do. When she saw that everyone was doing the Cowboy Hustle, one of the easier dances, she joined in. She turned her right foot out to the side and back, tapped her right heel and toe, kicked forward with her left and stepped back with her right, did the grapevine, quarter turn, a diagonal step, and started over.

At the end of the line dance, Jenna went to the head table where Carla and Bruce were taking a breather. Both looked flush from all the dancing they'd been doing.

"I just want to express my happiness for both of you and I need to see your engagement ring, Carla." Carla had told her the diamond was huge but hadn't been able to show her because of it being resized.

Carla held out her left hand. On her ring finger was a sizeable solitaire set in a diamond band.

"Wow, that is big," Jenna admired. "I've never seen a solitaire that large." She turned to Bruce. "You certainly have good taste in rings."

"Well, I can't take all the credit. When I told Monica I wanted to marry Carla, she agreed to come with me to look for the perfect ring for her sister. According to the jeweller, the band is 'made of channel-set diamonds which, with the solitaire, makes a stunning show of light.'"

"Well, it certainly does sparkle," Jenna agreed. She pulled her cell phone from her purse and snapped some pictures of the couple and the ring. She then turned and took a few of the whole room.

At eleven o'clock, finger sandwiches, cheese and crackers, vegetables, cold seafood and sauces, and a chocolate fountain surrounded by fruit and small squares of pound cake were set out. Jenna groaned because she hadn't yet worked off her supper but she stood to go join the others to sample what was there.

"Do you want anything?" she asked Adam.

"No, I'm fine."

Jenna decided to freshen up before eating and headed out into the hallway to find the washrooms. She was about to round a corner when she heard raised voices.

"I want to leave," a man said. "I don't know anyone and it's boring."

"You can't leave me here alone," a woman answered. "How do you think that will look?"

"I don't care. I have better things to do."

"Have you taken any pictures like I asked?"

"No. There's enough people taking pictures. You can get some from them."

Jenna didn't know if she should cough and act like she'd just come or if she should turn and leave. This wasn't something she wanted to walk in on.

"Why are you being like this?"

"I told you, the party is dull."

"Look. You're my fiancé and the least you could do is act like it."

Now Jenna recognized Monica's voice and she was arguing with Kevin. Jenna certainly sympathized with him. If you don't know any of the people at a party, it is hard to get into the mood. She decided to turn and leave. She went back into the ballroom and over to the lunch table.

When Jenna got back to the table with her plate full of chocolate-covered fruit, Adam wasn't there. She looked over at the bar area, thinking he had gone for another drink. He hadn't. She scanned the crowd and finally saw him talking with Mason again. She smiled. Maybe this evening was what Adam needed.

CHAPTER 2

$\mathcal{J}$enna closed the door of her condo and took off her shawl. She and Adam had left before the end of the engagement party, saying goodbye to Carla and Bruce, Hillary and Drake, and finally to each other outside the building. They then got into separate taxis to go home. She was glad that she didn't have to be at the bookstore until noon the next day. Knowing they would be out late, she and Adam had scheduled Michele to open.

She hung up her shawl and went into her bedroom to change into her nightgown. She then headed to her kitchen, found an open bag of chips, and dropped onto her couch in her living room. Jenna turned on her television and found the movie she had saved last week. She was tired but knew she wouldn't be able to get to sleep until she'd settled down after the evening's enjoyment.

Jenna was halfway through the movie when her cell phone rang. She pulled the phone from her purse and saw that it was Carla's number. She wondered what she would be calling about this late, on the night of her own engagement party. "Hello?"

"Oh, Jenna!" Carla cried. "You have to help us!"

"Carla, what wrong?" Jenna sat upright. "Are you hurt?"

"You have to come back!" Carla's voice sounded almost hysterical.

"What's happened?"

"Please, I'll explain it when you get here." Carla disconnected.

Jenna stared at the phone in her hand. When she and Adam had left, the party was going strong. The dance floor was full for every dance, most people were drinking but no one seemed to be getting drunk, and Carla and Bruce were holding hands as they wandered from one table to another visiting with their family and friends. What had changed? And why had Carla phoned her? Surely there were others who could help her.

Jenna wondered if she should get Adam to go with her. No, let him sleep. Whatever it was, no use in both of them going. She called a cab then changed into jeans and a sweater. She grabbed her black leather jacket and hurried down to the street to wait. A few minutes later, she was getting out of the taxi in front of the same door she'd exited just over an hour ago.

The band was packing its instruments into the back of a van and the caterers were loading up the left-over food in their cargo van. Jenna hastened into the building and to the door of the ballroom. The room was empty of guests. Some of the staff were pulling off the tablecloths and throwing them in large hampers on wheels. Others were stacking chairs on rolling platforms. The decorations had already been taken down.

Jenna looked around for Carla and saw her sitting in the same chair she had occupied behind the head table. She looked pale and was tearing bits off a piece of paper. Bruce sat beside her, head in his hands. This did not look good. Surely they hadn't had a fight after such a lovely evening.

When Carla saw her, she stood and rushed to Jenna, tears in her eyes. "Jenna, it's happening again!"

"What's happening again?" Jenna was confused.

Carla waved the tattered piece of paper in the air. "Someone is going to kill Bruce."

"What? Slow down." She glanced at Bruce who hadn't moved. "What do you mean?"

"This!" Carla shoved the note at Jenna.

Jenna took the note and looked at it. 'BRUCE DUMP HER OR DIE' was printed in capital letters in the centre of the paper. She looked into the frightened eyes of her friend and tried to keep her voice calm as she said. "Where did you find this?"

"It was on the table when we went to pick up our things to leave." Carla wrung her hands. "Oh, what are we going to do?"

"Where on the table? Beside your purse, under a champagne glass?"

Carla took the paper from Jenna, grabbed her arm, and pulled her to the table. She pointed to where Bruce sat. "Right there. It was tucked just under his plate." She demonstrated by pushing the note under the rim of the dish.

Bruce lifted his head to watch. Jenna felt sorry for him. His tie was off and the top button of his shirt open. He looked pale and miserable. Who wouldn't? He'd just been threatened. At his own engagement party. "Bruce, are you okay?"

Bruce nodded his head. "Just a little shaken." His voice was low. "This isn't what you expect from one of your guests, one of your friends."

"Was the note in an envelope?" Jenna asked him.

"No. Just folded and set there."

"Have you called the police?"

Bruce shook his head. "We talked about it but decided not to."

"Why?"

"What could they do? We don't know who left it."

Jenna looked at the crushed and frayed paper. She doubted that any fingerprints or DNA could be taken from it now. "It would be on record, though. So if anything else happens they would take it more seriously."

16

Bruce looked at Carla. "I guess we could take it to them tomorrow."

Carla nodded. "But I can't see any of our family or friends leaving it."

"It could have been one of the caterers, or one of the staff here," Jenna said.

"Yes, and with the guests that's over two hundred people for the police to check. I doubt they would bother."

"So, why did you call me?"

"Because you know my history with my past fiancés and you helped figure out who killed Hillary's employee, Bruno."

Jenna looked around the room. The catering staff was hovering, waiting to clean off the head table. "We should leave. I'll call a cab and we'll go to your condo, Carla."

They both nodded and gathered their things while Jenna took out her cell phone and hit redial for the cab company.

At Carla's condo, Carla and Bruce dropped side by side on the couch. They appeared deflated, all the happiness and delight of a few hours ago gone. Jenna went to the kitchen to make coffee. She didn't know if they wanted any but she needed some. She set three cups along with cream, sugar, and spoons on a tray and carried it to the coffee table in front of the couch. Bruce had his arm around Carla and her head was on his shoulder.

Jenna sat in one of the two overstuffed chairs and thought back to what she knew about her friend. Carla had been dating a man named Dale when Jenna had started working for her. They became engaged and began planning their wedding. Then one night, when Dale was leaving work, he was shot during what the police decided was a robbery. His empty wallet was found near his body. The killer was never found.

It had taken Carla three years to get over it and fall in love with another man: Roger. A day after he had given Carla a ring, Roger had gone out with some of his friends to celebrate his engagement. Sometime after he'd arrived home, he'd fallen off his fifth-storey apartment balcony. The police theorized he'd been leaning on the railing with his cell phone when he dropped it. They figured he made a grab for it and over-centered.

Last spring, Carla had come to see Jenna in her capacity as a dating coach. It had been ten months since Roger's death and she was tired of being alone. However, one thing bothered her. How and when could she tell a guy that her last two fiancés died before they could get married?

"I'm just wondering if I should put it in the comments," Carla had said. "That way they know about it from day one and I don't waste time on a guy who gets scared off when he finds out."

Jenna nodded. "Choosing how much information to give out on a dating site is a tough decision. No one wants a surprise declaration on a third date, just when you're thinking about inviting them to bed."

"So what do you advise?"

"In my opinion, I don't think you should put it up on the dating sites. And I don't think you should mention it on the first date. It would almost sound as if you are expecting the new relationship to end in an engagement."

"So when?"

"It could come up casually on the second date."

"When on the date?"

"Towards the end of the evening. That way he will have gotten to know you over the two dates and he could then decide if he likes you enough to continue seeing you in spite of the tragedies of your past."

They set up her profile on a site and a month later, Carla had come to her again. "Tonight is my second date with Bruce Everett. You said I could tell him about what happened to my two fiancés on our second date."

Jenna leaned her arms on her desk and looked at her client. "Yes, I did. But only if you feel comfortable enough with him to mention them after one date. Do you?"

"I don't know. We had a lot of fun together and we've been texting every day since."

"Do you think this relationship is ready for such a revelation?"

"He's told me about being in a five-year relationship which ended last year."

"That's promising. If he has opened up about something that personal then I think it would be okay for you to tell him about your fiancés."

"I hope the news doesn't scare him off," Carla said, as she left Jenna's office.

It obviously hadn't because tonight she'd attended their engagement party, just six months after they'd met. So why did it seem like someone wanted to break them up?

Jenna picked up a cup and took a small sip of the hot liquid. "So tell me exactly what happened."

Carla straightened up and Bruce dropped his arm. "We were gathering up our things, my purse, some cards we were given, the envelope with the receipt from paying the caterers." She paused and looked at Bruce. "What else was there?"

"My tie which I'd taken off, the bouquet of flowers we were taking with us as a souvenir. I think that's all." Bruce reached in his pocket and pulled out the note. He laid it in the centre of the table.

"And who found this?" Jenna took out her cell phone and snapped some pictures of the note.

"I did," Carla said. "I noticed it partially under Bruce's plate. I thought it was a congratulation note so I opened it." She stopped and shivered. Bruce put his arm around her again.

"Did anyone else see it?" Jenna asked.

"Everyone who was at the table. We were all packing up and saying goodbye at the same time. They all saw me find it and I'm afraid I didn't react very well."

"They were very concerned but we asked them all to keep it quiet," Bruce said. He finally took a drink from his cup.

"Well, there were a lot of people taking pictures. We could ask everyone at the party to look at their pictures and see if they may have caught someone hanging around the table."

"I don't think I want them to know about this," Carla said, slowly.

"Why?"

"I don't need all the questions, the condolences, the worry, everything that will be expressed by everyone. It'll just be too draining right now."

Jenna nodded in understanding. Two hundred phone calls, texts, or emails to the guests would be overwhelming. But that didn't leave them much. "What if you tell them you want to look at their photos to pick out a few for your wedding album?"

"That would work," Carla said, thoughtfully. "We didn't hire a photographer for this so it would make sense. We could send out messages and ask."

1"You'd have to tell them you want all photos," Jenna said. "That way they won't go through and pick out the ones they think you'll like. We don't want them deleting any."

"Good point. We should do that soon, then. What about the security cameras at the Convention Centre?"

"We can't just walk in and ask for them. We'd have to get the police to ask for them and they would probably need to get a warrant. I'm not sure if this note would be enough to get that warrant."

Jenna had a lot more questions but she wasn't sure if now was the right time to ask them. Maybe she should let Carla and Bruce sleep on it and ask them tomorrow. They might be better able to think through what the threat might mean and who could have made it. "Do you want to wait until tomorrow to discuss this further? I could come back in the morning."

Carla sighed and looked at Bruce. "I think that would be best. We've been working hard these past few weeks to plan this party and we're very tired. I can barely think straight."

Jenna stood. "Okay, I'll be here about ten o'clock."

Back at her condo, Jenna changed into her nightgown again and carried her cell phone to bed. Her body was tired but her mind was too active for sleep. She opened her photos and checked through the pictures she'd taken. There weren't many, just enough for her to have a record of the event.

CHAPTER 3

*C*arla closed the door behind Jenna and leaned against it. She felt the tears begin to fall. Why was this happening to her again? Who was doing this? When had she made such an enemy? Because she must have somewhere in her life for this to be occurring. It just couldn't be coincidence that two of her fiancés had died and now her third one was being threatened. It just couldn't.

Carla walked back to the living room. Bruce had picked up the tray with the empty cups and cream and sugar and carried it to the kitchen. He came back and put his arms around her. She leaned into him and rested her head against his shoulder. "Oh, Bruce, what are we going to do?"

"I'm beat but I don't think I'll be able to sleep. Let's go through the pictures we took to see if we can see something on them that we didn't notice during the party."

"Good idea. It will keep us busy for a while. But I'm going to change first."

Carla went to her bedroom. She slipped out of her dress and put on her housecoat. She walked into the ensuite and gasped at the image looking back at her in the mirror. Her hair was dishevelled, her tears had smudged her mascara down her cheeks, and her eyes looked haunted. As she wiped her make-up off and applied moisturizer, she wondered how Bruce was really taking this.

Would he want to call the whole thing off? She wouldn't blame him if he did. She had told him about her past engagements and the deaths of her fiancés while they were on their second date. At first, he seemed hesitant about dating her again but after three days had phoned her. They'd continued seeing each other and she'd soon fallen in love with him but hadn't been sure of his feelings until he took her skiing in Whistler. He'd said he loved her while they were on a ski lift. She'd been so elated. When he proposed, she asked him if he was sure he wanted to, given her history. He said he didn't believe in good or bad luck, karma, fate, or whatever you wanted to call it. She'd been so relieved.

But now...

Carla walked back to the living room. Bruce was still on the couch, his cell phone in his hand. He looked up and smiled at her.

"I'm looking at my pictures," he said. "And I'm not seeing anyone who doesn't belong there and nothing out of the ordinary."

Carla dug her phone out of her purse and brought up her photos. She hadn't taken many pictures during the evening and it didn't take her long to go through them. "None on mine, either."

Carla thought back to the evening and what she could remember of the people who had come and gone around the table. Some came to congratulate them or to talk with their attendants and the catering staff removed the supper plates and glasses and tried to keep the table tidy. Surely it had to have been left near the end of the evening or it would have been noticed earlier. Could it have been one of the catering or the convention centre's staff? But why? She didn't know any of them. And the rest were family and friends. Surely none of them disliked her enough to do this.

Carla flopped down beside Bruce. "What's going on?"

"I don't..." He didn't finish his sentence.

Carla turned to him. He was staring at his cell phone. He looked at her with a grimace.

"What? Did you find something?"

He didn't answer, just handed his phone to her.

Carla looked at the screen. It showed a Facebook post by someone named DeadGuy. It had been shared to Bruce's page by Bill.

The post showed a picture of them at the head table and read: *Carla is engaged for the third time. Will Bruce back off now that he's received a death threat or will he die like her two previous fiancés?*

Carla turned in horror to Bruce. "Who is this DeadGuy? Who wrote it?"

"I don't know," Bruce said. "I'm not friends with him."

"Why would Bill repost this on your page for all our family and friends to see?"

"That, I don't know, either. But I'll delete it and then find out."

Carla went on Facebook. The same post was on her page. She clicked on the three dots on the right top corner of the post. Up came a list of what she could do with it.

"Damn, there is no delete option to choose," Bruce said. "I can only hide it from my timeline. Now I'm going to call Bill and find out what the hell he's doing." He punched in a number on his phone.

"I can't delete it, either." Carla tried to keep her voice steady. "And even if I hide it, a message tells me that it may still appear in other places. She looked at Bruce. "What other places?"

"I don't know." Bruce shook his head. He put his phone on speaker and they listened to the dial tone. Finally, a voice came on telling him to leave a message.

"What's with the post on Facebook, Bill? Everyone promised they wouldn't repeat anything about the note. Call me." He pushed the end button and threw his phone on the table.

24

Carla leaned against him and Bruce put his arm around her shoulder.

"We'll find out who's behind this and why Bill would post that." Bruce shook his head. "I can't believe he would do this to me, to us."

Carla didn't know Bill very well. Even though Bruce and Bill had been friends for years, Bill hadn't attended many of their parties or gone out with them for a drink very often. When he did show up, he barely spoke to her. She had asked Bruce about it and he said he didn't have any idea what Bill's problem was.

"What if it's up on other social media sites like Instagram?" Carla asked.

"Oh, god."

They were silent for a while then Bruce yawned. "This isn't getting us anywhere. We should get some sleep."

"Are you staying the night?" He usually didn't, preferring to be at home in the morning when he woke up.

"I do want to be here when Jenna comes tomorrow. I want to hear what ideas she might have."

Sunday morning, Jenna showed up at Carla's condo on time. She wasn't sure if either Carla or Bruce would want to eat but she'd stopped for coffees and raisin bran muffins on the way. Carla buzzed Jenna into the building. When she opened the door at Jenna's knock, Carla was dressed in a long, flowing, pink housecoat. Her hair was messed and there were dark circles under her eyes. Jenna doubted she'd slept much. Bruce sat at the dining room table. He had on a pair of jeans and blue t-shirt. His suit and shirt were draped over the back of the couch. He obviously hadn't gone home. This must be hard on him, knowing what had happened to the previous men in his position.

Jenna was glad she'd brought some food to eat. They looked as if they could use something.

"So what do you think about the note this morning? Do you think it might be a prank?" she asked, as she set her cardboard tray of take-out coffee cups and bag of muffins on the table. There was no use making small talk.

Carla paused as she reached for plates in the cupboard. She glanced at Bruce.

Jenna noticed the look. Something had happened since she left them earlier this morning. "What's going on?"

"Show her, Bruce." Carla took out the plates and grabbed some cutlery and napkins from a drawer.

Bruce passed over a slip of paper. "I copied this from a post sent to both mine and Carla's Facebook pages by Bill. There was also a picture of us at the head table."

"*Bruce, I found this and thought you might want to see it,*" Jenna read the words Bill had written at the top of the message then looked down at the original post, "*Carla is engaged for the third time. Will Bruce back off now that he's received a death threat or will he die like her two previous fiancés?*" She stared at Bruce. "That's Bill, one of your trio and your second best man?"

"Yes. We couldn't delete them but we hid the posts so no one would read them."

"I thought everyone agreed they wouldn't tell anyone."

Jenna passed each of them a cup of coffee and put the muffins and small containers of butter on a plate. She took a picture of the copy of the post.

"They did. I phoned him last night to ask where he found it and why he'd reposted it to my page but he didn't answer. I left a message and he called this morning and said that he didn't know what I was talking about. He hadn't sent anything to me and he hadn't even seen it. He thinks maybe he's been hacked."

Jenna glanced from Bruce to Carla. "Do you know who DeadGuy is?"

They both shook their heads. "I've never seen any posts from him," Bruce said. "And so far no one has mentioned seeing the post so hopefully we got rid of it in time."

"But we don't know if it's up on other sites," Carla said.

Jenna scrolled down her Facebook page and didn't find anything. She checked her notifications and it didn't show up. "I don't see it anywhere on mine."

"That's good," Carla breathed. "It's no secret what happened to my past fiancés but I don't need someone turning Bruce and my engagement into a melodrama."

"I guess the note isn't a secret anymore," Bruce said.

"Maybe having it out in the open might make someone come forward," Carla said.

"Well, it certainly will make asking questions easier," Jenna agreed. The Facebook post was frightening for two reasons. First, the person was concealing their identity so it could be anyone and second, it sounded like the person wanted to stir things up in both Carla and Bruce's lives. Like they were doing this for their own enjoyment or maybe for revenge.

Jenna decided to change the subject. "Did you look through your photos from last night?"

"Yes, but we didn't find anything unusual," Bruce said. "What about you?"

"Nothing in mine, either. Did you contact your family and friends about seeing theirs?"

"That's what we have been doing this morning. We asked them to send them by email or put them on a USB stick. Some complained because they had taken so many and said they would pick out the best ones. It took some begging to get them to agree to send all they had to us. And without everyone knowing why we want the pictures, it'll take some time for them to get around to it and there will be a lot to go through."

"So, no one else beside the ones at the head table saw the note. You didn't show it to anyone?" Jenna took a sip of her coffee and picked up a muffin and a plate. She was hungry.

"No." Carla said. "We found it and I called you immediately."

"Did any of them see anyone come near the table during the night who shouldn't have been there." Jenna had gone over what she'd noticed the night before and nothing had stood out. People milled in groups all around the room. Couples danced. Single people strolled alone out into the hall, to the bar, to join a group. It had been a normal party.

Carla shook her head. "They were all as shocked as we were." She took a muffin and set in on her plate. "There was the catering staff. They were constantly coming around clearing our used plates and cutlery and replenishing our water glasses all night."

"Then it had to have been left there near the end of the night," Jenna mused. "Because there were still some dishes on the table when I got there."

"Yes, plus I'm sure someone would have seen it if it had been left earlier."

"Do you think this is connected with Dale and Roger's deaths?" Bruce asked.

28

Jenna paused in lifting her cup to her lips. She studied Carla and Bruce. This was something she had thought about but hadn't wanted to bring it up in front of Bruce. "What makes you ask that?"

"I don't know. It just doesn't seem like a coincidence."

"The police ruled that Dale's death was during a robbery and Roger's was an accident. This is a threat."

"But isn't it strange that two of her fiancés die and now I am told to get out of her life as soon as I'm a fiancé?"

"Why warn you and not the others?" Jenna asked.

"They could have been warned and didn't tell anyone."

Jenna looked at Carla.

Carla shook her head. "Neither mentioned anything."

"They might not have taken them seriously," Bruce said.

Carla's hand flew to her mouth. She stared at Jenna with wide eyes. "Oh, my. What if they did get one? What if their silence got them killed?"

"That's only speculation on our parts." Jenna put her hand on Carla's arm. "We don't know for sure they got a note before they died. The police never found one."

"Maybe they threw them away," Bruce said.

This was getting them nowhere. "I don't think this is connected to the others," Jenna said. "I'm not ruling it out but I think this is different. Someone wants you out of the picture, not dead." And now the tough question. "Do you have any idea who would have written this?"

"We've talked about it and there's no one we can think of," Bruce said, while Carla shook her head.

"Who were your guests? Family, friends, business contacts? How do you know them?"

"Mine were family, friends, employees, and a couple of franchise owners," Carla said.

"Mine too," Bruce agreed.

"Any ex-boyfriends or girlfriends, anyone you've had a disagreement with and then patched up? Someone who might still be holding a grudge of some sort?"

Carla and Bruce looked thoughtfully at each other and then at Jenna.

"No," Carla said. "I can't recall any disputes I've had with any of my guests that would cause them to do something like this. And as we know, my two exes are dead."

"I didn't invite any of my exes and like Carla, I don't think I've had a disagreement with anyone that would make them mad enough to do this."

"Did you notice a stranger or someone you hadn't invited?"

"Well, I don't know all of Bruce's guests and he doesn't know all of mine," Carla said. "And we didn't have a receiving line so there could have been someone who showed up that we would have thought was the other's guest."

"So basically you have to look at the pictures that come in and acknowledge which ones each of you know. That way if there is one neither of you recognize, it could be the person."

"That's going to be a lot of work," Bruce said.

"This may be difficult to hear but someone at the table had a better chance of leaving this than anyone else," Jenna said. "Are the ones at the head table the same ones who will be in your wedding party?"

"Yes," they both said, in unison.

"They were introduced last night by their first names and their relationship to each of you was explained. I'm going to have to speak with all of them. Can you give me their full names and phone numbers so I can talk with them?

"We thought you might ask for them," Bruce said. "I have their info here." He produced a piece of paper from his shirt pocket and handed it to Jenna.

Jenna looked at the list: Monica Bell, Lillian Homan, Rachael Campbell, Ronnie Simpson, Bill Black, Mason Devers."

"We can rule out Monica," Carla said, emphatically. "And Lillian and Rachael, too. I've known Rachael for years and Lillian is my cousin."

"Tell me more about them." Jenna folded the paper and put it in her pocket.

"Rachael and I knew each other in middle school and high school and worked together at the same print shop while going to university. She studied archaeology and has spent the years since travelling the world working on digs. Occasionally, I've taken a holiday to the country where she was and she would show me the sites.

"When she is in town between excavations, we spend as much time together as possible. She's visiting with her family then leaving next week to go back to a dig in England. Lillian's father and my mother were brother and sister. We spent time together as kids at family gatherings but drifted apart for a while. She works for an import-export company in Surrey."

"And you can rule out my best man and groomsmen too. Ronnie, Bill, and I have been friends since we were kids. We have gone through a lot together and none of us would turn on another. Mason is my cousin. His mom and my dad are siblings.

"He and his younger sister used to come and visit with their parents. I don't know what she did while at our place but Mason used to hang with Ronnie, Bill, and me. He was quiet but usually went along with most of our dumb ideas. He's family."

Carla's phone rang. She looked at the number and grimaced. "My cousin," she said to Jenna and Bruce. "I'd better take it or she'll just keep calling." She swiped to accept the call. "Hello, Lillian."

Carla listened. "I'm okay. You don't have to come over. Bruce and my friend Jenna are here. Jenna brought coffee and muffins." Carla paused and listened. "I don't need anything and I have to go. Bye."

Carla hung up and smiled weakly at Jenna. "Sorry. She was getting insistent."

Jenna smiled back but her mind was digesting the abrupt way Carla had handled the conversation. She wondered at the unfriendly tone in Carla's voice, especially after Carla had insisted that Lillian had nothing to do with the note. Was there something amiss in their relationship that Carla wasn't admitting? Jenna had thought they must be close in order for Carla to ask Lillian to be a bridesmaid. But Lillian had called her to offer her help and Carla had been curt with her. They may be cousins but it didn't sound like they were friends. So, why was she a bridesmaid? Maybe Lillian was someone she should speak with first.

She checked her watch. She didn't have time for any more now. "I have to get to the bookstore," she said, standing.

"Thank you so much for coming this morning and for the goodies." Carla walked Jenna to the door. "Just knowing that you are on our side and will find out who left the note makes me feel much better than I did last night."

Jenna didn't know if she liked that. It was a lot of pressure and she had absolutely no idea what to do. There was nothing to go on right now. "Let me know when you get some pictures. Maybe they will show something."

Carla nodded. "Will Adam be helping you?"

"Adam?" Jenna asked, in surprise.

"Yes. You two seem to work well together and I'd feel better if there are two of you on this. I'd hate for something to happen to you."

"That sounds a bit ominous."

"Well, if it has anything to do with Roger and Dale's deaths, it might be."

"You should tell that to the police, also."

Carla nodded.

CHAPTER 4

Jenna drove under the south end of the Granville Street Bridge, onto Granville Island, and parked in her spot. She walked the block to the light blue building, with a rusty-red tower, known as the Net Loft. Inside, she worked her way through the crowd of shoppers towards her bookstore, peeking at various shop displays as she went. That was one of the reasons she and Adam had chosen to buy the bookstore in this building. Each business had large windows to display their latest acquisitions. She and Adam always kept their exhibitions up to date with new releases and weekly discount sales.

"Good morning, Sophia," Jenna said, holding the door of the bookstore open for the older woman stepping out with a bag full of books. All of the stores in the loft had double doors and most of them only had one open during the day. She and Adam kept both their doors closed to keep their cats from wandering away. Not that lazy Maggie or skittish Trish had ever tried to escape, but they didn't want to take the chance.

"Morning, Jenna," Sophia said.

Sophia had on her usual orange cardigan over khaki pants and a yellow blouse. Her short, white hair was hidden under a wide hat. Jenna noted that she'd traded her hiking boots for running shoes. Sophia Bouvier and her sister, Edna Robison, lived on a houseboat moored to the island. They researched past murders and wrote true crime novels. They'd done a reading and signing of their latest book at the store a few months ago that had been very successful. Last spring, the sisters had decided to venture into fiction.

"How is your mystery novel coming?" Jenna asked.

"We're finding it's harder to think up a crime and sprinkle clues than it is to research a true crime and write all the facts." Sophia held up her bag. "Got more books to read to see how other writers do it."

Jenna let the door close and bent to rub Maggie's ears. Maggie was a long-haired, orange tabby and one of the two cats who lived in the store. She set herself up on a chair near the door each morning and expected a pet from everyone entering or leaving the store, protesting loudly if anyone ignored her. She was very popular with the regular customers and a bit of a shock to the new ones.

"Good morning," Jenna said to Adam, who was behind one of the cash registers at the u-shaped counter.

"Morning," he smiled, as he rang up a sale.

Michele was helping a woman look for a cookbook. After her initial shock at being suspected in the death of her boyfriend last spring, Michele had thought about quitting her job and moving back to her hometown of Calgary, Alberta, but she'd changed her mind after her mother told her about the late spring snowstorm the city had received and the almost record-setting cold snap.

Jenna and Adam were both happy with her decision to stay.

Jenna headed to the back. The bookstore itself was one large room, but the back was made up of smaller rooms containing an office, washroom, and two storage rooms, one of which they used as a lunch/staff room. She and Adam were proud of how they had taken the run-down business with its dilapidated shelves, older books, and faded paint and turned it into the success it was today.

They'd spent a month painting walls, building new shelves, organizing the shelves for maximum exposure of each book, ordering new releases and sorting them according to genre and then author, and had changed the name from Raymond's Books to A Novel Bookshop.

On their big opening day, they'd been overwhelmed by the number of customers and had sold out many of the new releases they'd purchased. They'd also hosted many events to encourage customers to visit the store, like book readings by local, aspiring, and bestselling authors and a children's corner. They allowed book clubs and writing groups to gather and had established a Writers Teach Writing course. There was something happening every day that kept them busy.

In the office, Jenna put her purse in the safe and checked the schedule for her Sunday client. Soon after they'd bought the bookstore, with Adam's approval, she began using their office as her dating coach consulting workspace. She'd started her coaching business because her friends, and their friends, had thought she was an expert on dating and dating sites.

Sure, she'd been using the sites for a few years and yes, she had met some really nice guys, as well as some strange, eccentric, and angry ones, but she was still single. Not a good advertisement. However, that hadn't stopped people from coming to her for advice. Invariably, they began the conversation with: 'You've had a lot of practice at filling out the dating site questionnaires and have met a lot of men …'

Even though she protested that it hadn't been that many sites and that many men, they continued with their questions. She'd checked into the requirements needed to become a dating coach and found that the profession wasn't licensed. She learned coaches offered advice as well as direction and training in how to act on dates. With her degree in sociology, where she'd studied the culture of everyday life, the patterns of human relationships, and the social interactions of men and women, plus her dating site experiences, she decided she was qualified to set up business as a dating coach. She did consulting on the etiquette of the first date, second date, and even third date—if it was necessary. Or, if her client was very nervous, she would do an actual date simulation. For a male or lesbian client she would act as his/her prospective date and she would give pointers on how to dress, how to carry on a conversation, how to flirt and, when it was appropriate, how to touch. If the client was a woman or a gay man, she hired Adam to act as the first date. She would sit nearby and give advice on the same topics.

Jenna even coached a few on the old-fashioned way of meeting people: grocery shopping, walking a dog, or going to a library. In the past two years, she'd helped many clients meet their perfect mate and had been invited to one wedding.

She had a website advertising her business and a blog where she discussed the many and various phases of dating and even how to successfully break up with a boyfriend or girlfriend. Today's client wouldn't arrive until two-thirty, so she went back up to the front. Michele's shift would be over in a few minutes.

Jenna stepped up beside Adam to bag the books he had just sold, thanking the customer for coming.

"You look tired," Adam said. "Didn't sleep well?"

Jenna looked around to see if anyone was near. She leaned closer. "Carla phoned me last night from the conference centre. Someone put a note on the head table telling Bruce to leave her or he would die."

"What?" Adam gaped at her. "You're kidding me, right?"

Jenna pulled her cell phone from her pocket and opened her photos. She showed the note to Adam.

Adam whistled. "That must have been a shock to them."

"It was. They were both pretty shaken when I got there. We cabbed it to Carla's place and talked a bit but they were too tired to make sense of it. I went back this morning."

"Do they have any idea who would have written it?"

"No. All the people who were there were family and friends."

"Sometimes people we think are friends, actually aren't."

"Yes," Jenna nodded. She wondered if Adam was thinking of his last boyfriend who had told him so many lies during their relationship.

"How many know about this note?"

"So far, only the ones at the head table. They were all there when Carla found it. But she and Bruce swore them to secrecy because they don't want to go through the aggravation of having all their guests contacting them to wish them well."

"I know this is awful to say," Adam said, pensively. "But have they thought about it being related to the deaths of Carla's previous fiancés?"

"Yes, we did discuss it but we couldn't figure out how. One was murdered, one died in an accident, and this one gets a note." Jenna waved to Michele who was leaving the store.

"Well, if they are related, the killer got away with murder twice, "Adam said. "Maybe the person is getting scared that they may make a mistake and get caught by killing Bruce. Maybe they think if they can scare him off, it would be just as good."

"A killer with cold feet," Jenna mused. "Usually once they've gotten away with murder, they like doing it and want to carry on. They think they're smarter than the police and enjoy taunting them. It's not likely this person would stop after the second one."

A couple came to the counter with some books. Adam talked with them while he scanned the purchases and Jenna bagged them. There were still some shoppers browsing the shelves.

"Are Carla and Bruce going to show the note to the police and explain everything?" Adam asked, as he leaned against the counter.

"Yes, today. But the note is so tattered and has been handled so much that I don't think the police can do anything with it, if they decide it's worth looking into at all."

Jenna reached under the counter and picked up the cat treat tin. She shook it and Trish, their black and white cat, zipped around the corner of the counter to get her share. Trish was shy and usually hid under the counter or in one of the back rooms during the day. They didn't always know where she was but they knew how to get her to come out. Maggie stood and stretched then jumped off the chair and sauntered over. Jenna dropped some treats onto the floor for each of the cats then put the lid on and placed it back on the shelf. Trish gulped her treats down while Maggie ate hers daintily.

"And without the police there is no way they can see any security camera footage," Adam said.

"Right. And there's more."

"More?"

"Yes. Someone posted a picture of them from last night on Facebook with this message." She showed the picture she had taken of what Bill had written.

"*Carla is engaged for the third time. Will Bruce back off now that he has received a death threat or will he die like her two previous fiancés?*" Adam read.

"It was first posted by someone who calls himself DeadGuy and shared to their pages by Bill."

"Bill? That seems like a nasty thing to put out there for everyone to read especially after agreeing to keep it quiet."

"Well, according to Bill he didn't share it. He claims he hadn't even seen it and thinks maybe his Facebook page has been hacked."

When Maggie finished her treats, she went back to the chair by the door and settled on the cushion. Trish curled up in a corner under the counter.

"So, why did they phone you about all this?" Adam asked.

"Well, for some reason they think we can find out who is behind this."

"We?"

"Yes. Carla made a point of saying that she would feel better with the two of us on their side. She has confidence that we will discover who sent the note."

"Well, that's just great." Adam threw his hands up in the air. "And how are we going to do that?"

"No idea." Jenna shrugged. "The only thing I could think of was to ask for the photos."

"I'll look through mine, also," Adam said. "But I didn't take very many."

Jenna grinned impishly at him. "So now you know as much as I do. What should we do next, my gumshoe buddy?"

Adam was saved from answering by a customer coming to the counter. He made a face at Jenna as he turned to the person.

CHAPTER 5

"You can stay, you know," Carla said to Bruce. She hoped he would agree but knew he wouldn't.

"I really have to get back to my place. I need to shower and change and meet Ronnie. We have to go over some business papers before signing them. Plus, I want to take this note to the police and see what they have to say."

Carla nodded. She knew about the big deal Bruce and Ronnie had been working on for three months. If everything went well, they would begin construction on a craft brewery in Whistler this fall. They were both excited about it since it was their first joint business venture. And it would be nice for Bruce's peace of mind if the police could help find who put the note on the table.

Carla kissed Bruce goodbye and closed the door. She showered and, as she dressed in slacks and sweater, she asked herself the questions that had been plaguing her mind since last night. Who could be doing this? Someone from her past? Someone who resented her success? There were a few people she could think of but did they hate her enough to threaten her fiancé?

Carla went to the kitchen and cleaned the plates and cutlery off the table. It had been nice of Jenna to bring the muffins and coffee. Neither Carla nor Bruce had thought about eating. They'd been so shaken by what had happened and caught up in trying to figure out who would do this and why.

Once she'd gotten over the initial shock of finding the note the night before, she'd thought of Jenna. They'd been friends for years and Jenna had been so helpful at getting her back in the dating scene. She answered her every question and had been the person who quelled Carla's fears about dating again. The rest of the head table had suggested calling the police but she had resisted. Jenna would know what to do, she had thought.

Again, her mind went to who would have left the note and two names came to her. But how? Why?

Carla's phone rang. She picked it up. "Hi, Monica."

"How are you doing this morning?"

"A little better."

"Do you want me to come over? I can be there in half an hour."

"Thanks but I was thinking of going over to Mom's and telling her about the party and the note."

Carla had been so disappointed when her mother hadn't been able to make the engagement party because of a recently broken leg but she had vowed to make sure Becky attended the wedding. Now, she wasn't sure if there was still going to be a wedding because someone seemed determined to prevent it.

"Any idea who might have left it?"

"No, not yet, but Jenna is helping me."

"Well, you know who I think it is. Roberta and Conrad are the only ones we know who begrudge us any happiness."

"Yes, I was just thinking of them and I'm going to ask mom about them when I get there."

"Good. Let me know if there is anything I can do."

Carla dialed her mother's number. "Hi, Mom. Do you want some company this afternoon?"

She listened.

"Okay, I'll see you later."

She wanted to talk to her mother about the two people who might dislike her enough to print the note: Roberta and Conrad. Because as far as she knew, Bruce didn't have any enemies.

42

CHAPTER 6

"So, who's this Dorothy that Mason mentioned last night?" Jenna asked Adam, as they relaxed on the stools behind the counter. "You've never told me you have a friend named Dorothy."

"I don't," Adam laughed. "It's gay slang."

"Gay slang? For what?"

"To find out a person's sexual orientation."

"Oh?" Jenna raised her eyebrows waiting for an explanation.

"During World War II, homosexual acts were illegal in the United States, so if a man asked another man if he was a friend of Dorothy's, he was actually asking if he was gay."

"Why Dorothy?"

"Well, there are two theories to that. One is about Dorothy Parker who was a writer and socialite in the 1920s and 1930s. She was married to a bisexual man and was a defender of human rights. She would have parties where many of the invited guests were gay. They would use the phrase in order to gain entry."

"And the other?"

"The other is from *The Wizard of Oz.*"

"What?"

"Yes, if you look at the movie Dorothy is accepting of those who are different. Judy Garland actually became an icon for the gay community after that film. And there is another term used. Are you a friend of Mrs. King? Mrs. King, obviously meaning 'Queen', which is one of the terms for a gay man."

Jenna shook her head. "I didn't know all this."

"Most straight people don't."

The bell over the door clanged. Jenna looked over and smiled. She recognized the man who entered as her two-thirty client from the picture he'd sent. She held out her hand. "I'm Jenna."

He took her hand. "Ray Weaver."

"Come back to my office." Jenna led the way through the rows of shelves. She opened the door and entered, holding it for Ray to follow her.

"Please, sit." Jenna indicated the chair in front of her desk. She sat behind the desk and looked at him. He was about thirty-five, medium height, with sandy, blond hair and blue eyes. "So, give me an idea about your dating history."

"Not much to tell," Ray shrugged. He seemed nervous, which was natural. Most of the men who came to her were uneasy about admitting they were having trouble with dating. "I've had a few girlfriends but nothing lasted very long."

Hmm, a man of few words. This could be harder than she thought. "Have you ever been married?"

"No."

Okay, no exes to get in the way. "Any children?"

"No."

Better. No extra baggage. The big question was why? Usually by his age there was some history of a serious romance somewhere. "Have you ever been in a long-term relationship?"

"No."

Jenna was getting worried. What was wrong with this man, other than being very unforthcoming with information? Was that the reason women didn't stay around very long—that he didn't seem to know much about communication? She hoped that wasn't his problem because there was no way she could help him correct that. It would take a lot of sessions with a professional.

"So tell me, how you have met women in the past?" She mentally dared him to answer that with one word.

"Well, I dated my high school sweetheart for a couple of years. Then I met a woman through my brother and we went out for about a year. My last girlfriend was three years ago. We dated for about two months."

Well, he did know how to talk. "Did you see anyone between those women?" Maybe he just needed to relax a little.

"A few times but usually for only one date."

"So, why have you come to me?" She always asked this question. She wanted to know if they expected a miracle because she was a dating coach.

"You don't remember me, do you?" Ray asked.

Jenna took a good look at him. She couldn't place him. She shook her head.

"I'm Aubree's brother. I was one of the groomsmen at her and Brock's wedding."

"Oh, yes. Aubree and Brock." Two people who had met as a result of her coaching and whose wedding she'd been invited to. It had been a lovely occasion and she had a vague memory of who had stood up with them. "Didn't you have a moustache at the time?"

"Yes," Ray grinned. "I decided to get rid of it recently."

Jenna was glad to see the grin. He was becoming more and more human. He just had to loosen up.

"So, Aubree recommended me?" That was nice. Word of mouth was great advertisement.

"Yes. She told me you work magic."

"Well, not magic but I try my best."

"If you do half as good for me as you did for her, I'll be happy."

"Then, let's get to work. Do you have a profile on any dating sites that I can look at?"

"I've only gone on one." Ray dug out his cell phone and opened it.

At the same time, Jenna's cell phone pinged. She took it out of her pocket and glanced at it. It was a text from Carla. *I have some photographs to send you.*

Good. Busy now. Will text later. She shut her phone off so the pinging wouldn't bother them.

"This is what I put up." Ray handed his cell to her.

Jenna read through what he'd written and how he answered the questions. It seemed pretty normal. "I see you have your own business." That was always a good sign.

"Yes."

"'We Deal In What's Left Behind.' That's an unusual name. What does it mean?"

Here, Ray hesitated. "I go into homes and remove the furniture, clothing, papers, and all memorabilia after people have died."

"What?"

"I'm hired by families to go through the homes of relatives who have passed away and sort all their things into sell, give-away, or throw-away piles."

That sounded a little macabre, Jenna thought.

"It's a much-needed service," Ray said, as if reading her mind. "It takes the onus off the family to have to go through things that bring back memories of the person who died. When I'm finished they can sell the house without any hardship on their part."

"How long have you been in business?"

"Three years."

Ah, that might be where the problem was. "Have you had women answer you on this site?"

"Yes. I've talked to a few on the phone but none of them want to go out with me."

"Do you tell the women about your business?"

"Well, yes. What each of us do for a living is one of the topics we talk about."

"Okay, well I think that might be why you don't have dates. Maybe tell them that you own a moving company."

"They will still find out eventually, especially if they want to hire me to move them or someone they know and I have to decline."

"Yes, but by then they'll have had a chance to get to know you. I would suggest you go on two or even three dates before you explain exactly what type of moving you do. If you tell them in person they might understand it better." Jenna made a mental note for her next blog topic—could a person's job or career be a reason for not going on a date with them?

"Do you really think so?" For the first time, Ray's voice had some optimism in it.

"It's worth a try."

"Okay, can you give me some pointers on how to bring it up and how to describe it delicately?"

"If you want, we can do a mock date so you can practice on me. It's part of my service."

Ray's face brightened. "I'd like that."

Jenna checked her schedule and they made an appointment for the next weekend. She walked him through the bookstore to the door and said goodbye. She petted Maggie then turned on her phone as she went to the counter where Adam was pricing some second-hand books.

"So, how did it go?"

Jenna leaned on the counter. "He has a most unusual job that I think probably turns women off."

"What's that?"

"He goes into dead people's houses and removes all their stuff so the houses can be sold."

"Sounds ghoulish."

"Yes, but I guess for some people it's essential. Saves the family a lot of work and maybe sadness and gets the house cleaned out for resale."

Jenna's phone pinged. *Did you look at the photos I sent? There aren't many of them yet.*

Doing that now, Jenna sent back.

"Carla sent me some photos that were taken last night." She looked at Adam. "Did you see anyone hanging around the head table who looked nervous like they were doing something suspicious?"

Adam shook his head. "I wouldn't have known who was supposed to be there and who wasn't." He picked up the books and carried them to the used-book section.

Jenna scrolled through the twenty-nine pictures quickly, just to get a look at them. She would scrutinize them better later.

"See anything interesting?" Adam asked, coming back to the counter.

"Not so far. I'll have to look more closely when I get a chance."

A man and young boy came up to pay for their books.

"Hi, Mr. Bowers, Adrian." Jenna smiled down at the boy. "I missed you at the **Children's Reading Hour** yesterday."

The Children's Corner was a small area beside the children's book section. She and Adam had set up two little tables for children to sit at and read. It was here that Jenna held the reading hour every Saturday morning. She'd pick one or two books to read to the children and then they would have a discussion about them.

"I was at my grandma's." Adrian reached up and put two books on the counter. "It was her birthday."

"Oh, that must have been fun." Jenna rang up the sale. "Did you have cake?"

"Yes, there were two cakes, one white and one chocolate."

"And which one did you have?" Jenna accepted some bills from Mr. Bowers and gave him his change.

"I had a piece of each," Adrian said.

"Good for you." She put the books in a bag and handed it to Adrian. "I think I'd have done the same."

Jenna watched as Adrian petted Maggie before he and his dad left the store. Another customer entered and Jenna smile at her.

"What time do you close?" The woman asked.

"We close at six o'clock every day."

The woman looked at her watch. "Thank you." She headed towards the cooking section.

Jenna found the paper with the names and phone numbers of the wedding party and looked up Lillian's number. She dialed it and listened to it ring.

"Hello?"

"Lillian, My name is Jenna and I'm a friend of Carla's. She told me about the note found on the table last night and asked that I try to figure out who might have left it."

"Are you a detective?"

"No, just a friend."

"Then why did she ask you?"

Jenna wasn't sure how to answer that. She had no skills at detecting and although she'd managed to solve one mystery it didn't mean she could do it again. "She is pretty upset and needs someone to help her." Generic but maybe it would pass. "Did you see anyone around the table last night who shouldn't have been?"

"There were lots of people coming up to congratulate them. I didn't pay any attention to them. I spent most of my time dancing." She paused. "Is that why Carla asked for my photos?"

"Yes. We're hoping one of them might show someone leaving the piece of paper."

"Well, I sent the few I took to her. You can get them from her. Is there anything else?"

Jenna could understand Carla's reluctance to speak with Lillian. Jenna decided to be just as blunt as Lillian. "Why did Carla pick you for one of her bridesmaids?"

"What?"

"I just want to know your relationship with Carla."

"We're cousins. She and Monica are the only cousins I have. Actually, they're the only family I have since my parents died. Does that answer your question because I have to get ready to go out?"

That probably explained why she was in Carla's wedding party. "Thank you for your help." Jenna hung up.

They were busy for the rest of the afternoon. After the last customer left, Jenna hung the closed sign and locked the door. They took the money trays from the registers and headed to the office. Adam looked after the bookkeeping and paid the bills, while Jenna did the ordering of the books, magazines, novelties, and ornaments. It was a good arrangement for both.

When they'd counted the proceeds for the day and returned the floats to the trays, they locked everything in the safe. Tomorrow was Monday and, since Monday mornings were the slowest times of the week, they were usually the time when Adam did up the previous week's paperwork. Jenna looked after the store and dusted the counter and shelves and did a good vacuum of the floor. Each day, one of them gave the area near the door a quick sweep when it was needed.

"Want to go for a drink and something to eat at The Keg?" Jenna asked, as they shut off the lights and headed to the door.

"Only if you promise to show me the photos Carla sent."

"What? You mean I have to bribe you now to spend an evening with me?"

"Well, you know my time is valuable and my social life busy."

"Yeah, right. Just like mine." Jenna laughed. "That's why you had to accompany me to the engagement party last night."

CHAPTER 7

*C*arla used her key to open the door to her mother's apartment building. She rode the elevator to the ninth floor, again using her key to enter her mother's home. Carla's, Monica's, and their mother's lives hadn't always been as ideal as they were now. In their early childhood, everyday items like clothes that fit, enough food, and even a roof over their heads, had been sparse.

Their father had abandoned his family, leaving their mother, Becky, to raise the two sisters. Becky tried her best but couldn't get well-paying jobs and they moved into ever shoddier apartments. She visited the food bank to supplement their meals and they dropped in at a soup kitchen more times than Carla wanted to admit. Carla was embarrassed that she had to eat there but she also knew if she wanted a full belly, she had to swallow her pride.

Finally, Becky found steady work as a cleaner for a property management group. She went into businesses at night to dust desks and counters, disinfect bathrooms, and vacuum and wash the floors. For extra money, she even did some painting for the management group. She also had a part-time job cleaning apartments and houses after renters moved out.

When she was old enough, Carla had found a job at a fast-food restaurant and helped contribute to their finances while simultaneously keeping her grades up. She graduated high school and continued working to put herself through university. During that time she still lived at home to help her mother with payments. Monica also graduated high school and went to a dental assistant academy. She now worked for a very nice dentist and lived in an apartment not far from their mother's place.

One Saturday, when Carla was in her early twenties, Becky had invited both her daughters out for lunch. Carla was surprised because they seldom ate out. It was close to Christmas and as they walked past the soup kitchen where they used to eat Carla saw a man standing outside the door. He smiled and wished everyone Merry Christmas as he handed out wrapped gifts to the people walking into the building. The man's smile widened when he saw Becky and her daughters.

"So these are your girls, Becky," he said.

"Yes." Becky nodded. "Hayden, I'd like you to meet Carla and Monica. Girls, this is Hayden Saunders."

"So nice to finally meet you, Carla and Monica." Hayden held his hand out to Carla. "Your mother has told me so much about you both."

Carla slowly reached out and shook his hand. Who was this man and why had their mother talked about them to him? Monica also seemed hesitant as she shook Hayden's hand.

"Hayden is joining us for lunch," Becky said.

Hayden handed out his last two gifts and the four of them continued down the sidewalk to a Greek restaurant on the corner. Hayden and Becky talked about the weather but Carla and Monica were silent. Carla didn't know what to say and it seemed that Monica felt the same.

"Hayden is my new boss," Becky said when they were settled at a table and had the menus in front of them.

"New boss?" Carla asked. Her mother hadn't said anything about changing jobs.

"Yes," Becky said proudly. "He owns three shoe stores and I'm now the manager of one of them."

"Hey, congratulations." Carla leaned over and gave her mother a kiss on her cheek.

"Yes, congrats," Monica echoed. "Why didn't you tell us you were looking for a different job?"

"Well, it kind of happened out of the blue." Becky smiled at Hayden. "I clean one of Hayden's shops and sometimes he'd come in early before I was finished and we would talk. When his manager gave her notice, he asked me if I wanted the job. I jumped at the chance."

That seemed strange, Carla thought. Hayden offered her mother a job without any training. She wondered if there was something more.

"The previous manager is going to train me before she leaves," Becky continued, her face glowing.

Carla felt some relief at hearing that. Managing a business wasn't easy, having to deal with purchasing and sales, employees and hours, and disgruntled customers.

While they ate Hayden told them a little about himself. He was recently divorced with one son. He'd started out with one shoe store in a mall and had slowly increased the number to three across Vancouver.

Carla wasn't sure how long her mother had known Hayden before she started working for him but Hayden came for Christmas dinner that year and he and Becky went to Mexico together in January. By then Carla had seen the love they had for each other. When Carla moved out in the spring Becky gave her notice with her apartment manager and moved in with Hayden. They'd married in the summer.

Hayden had died last year and Becky now lived alone in the two bedroom apartment. Six months ago she sold the shops and had just opened a vintage clothing store.

"Come in, Carla."

Carla closed the door. To her left was the kitchen, and farther on was the dining room. The small, grey-haired woman was seated at the dining room table, a number of papers spread in front of her and a glass of white wine to the side. Her leg, in its fiberglass cast, was propped on a stool. She looked up and smiled at Carla. Carla bent and kissed her mother on her forehead. She sat in the chair across from Becky.

"How's your leg?"

"Still very sore. How was the party last night? Was it the success you'd hoped?" Becky straightened the papers into a pile.

"It was perfect until the end."

Becky stopped. "This sounds serious. Get yourself a glass of wine while I get comfortable in the living room."

Carla went to the kitchen cupboard and took out a glass. She found the opened bottle of wine in the fridge and poured some into the glass. Becky pushed herself up from the table.

"Do you want help?" Carla asked.

"No, I'm getting used to hobbling around with my crutches." She reached for the crutches propped against the wall and made her way to one of the chairs in the living room.

Carla picked up Becky's glass and carried it to the small end table beside the chair. She shoved a foot stool under her mother's leg then sat on the couch. The other furniture in the room was a television on the wall, a coffee table, and an old upright piano. Hayden used to play it when he was alive. There was also a gas fireplace with flames leaping from the artificial logs.

"So tell me."

Carla kept few secrets from her mother. She always went to her when she needed someone to listen. Her mother and Hayden had been the first ones she'd told when her first fiancé had died and she'd run to her mother at the death of her second fiancé. So it just seemed natural, after telling Becky about her engagement party, to launch into the last few minutes of it. When she was finished Becky was silent for a few minutes.

"How have you handled this so far?"

Carla told her about phoning Jenna, her dating coach, about the suggestions Jenna had made, the discussions she'd had with Jenna and Bruce, about Bruce taking the note to the police.

"It sounds like you've done as much as you can for now." Becky leaned forward. "Do you have any idea who would be doing this to you and Bruce?"

Carla hesitated.

"What?"

"Would this be something Roberta or Conrad might do?" She took a sip of her wine as she watched her mother's reaction.

"Oh." Becky sat back.

Roberta was Hayden's first wife and Conrad was their son. He'd been three when they divorced. Hayden had paid child support and alimony but Roberta had never been happy with the amount. She'd always been after Hayden for more and had even harassed Becky, saying that she was the one who stopped him from paying what he was supposed to.

In his will, Hayden left $20,000 to Conrad and Roberta received $5000. His share of the business and his life insurance was left to Becky. Roberta took Becky to court demanding more money for both of them, but the judge declined to grant her wish.

Since then, they'd hounded Becky, accusing her of convincing Hayden to lessen the amount of money they were to receive in his will and then killing him. They said that she'd stolen Conrad's inheritance and a settlement that Roberta should have received.

At first, Becky tried to convince them that Hayden had died of a heart attack and she had nothing to do with it. When that didn't work, she ignored them. Roberta and Conrad then went after Carla and Monica, leaving messages and sending letters telling them that their mother was a murderer and all the insurance money and business money Becky had inherited belonged to them when she died.

"Monica pointed out that they're the only ones who might want to spoil my happiness. After all, they've never liked us. The cards they sent to me after the deaths of Dale and Roger weren't ones of sympathy. They'd gloated at my sorrow, telling me it was what I deserved."

"They weren't invited to your party, though."

"I know." Carla nodded. "But no one was keeping track of the guests coming and going. One of them could have slipped in."

"Maybe they'll show up in one of the pictures. But I would think that if they went, they'd have been in some sort of disguise, like one of the caterers."

"And there were plenty of them in and out most of the evening," Carla said, ruefully. "When was the last time you heard from them?

"It's been a while." Becky held up her glass.

Carla smiled and stood. She took her own and Becky's glasses to the kitchen and refilled them. "The bottle is empty," she said, as she returned.

"There is another in the cupboard, if you want more."

"Thanks, but this is enough for me." Carla sat down. "So how long is a while?"

"It's been about six months since I've seen them. Not sure how long since they've lurked around watching me."

Carla remembered times that she'd seen Roberta or Conrad standing on a street corner near her office or waiting across the street when she came out of a restaurant.

"I've been thinking—no, hoping—that maybe they've given up," Becky continued.

"It would be nice. Maybe one of them found a rich lover."

"Pity that poor person," Becky smiled.

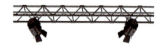

$\mathcal{J}$enna and Adam walked to the restaurant just down the street from the Net Loft. They entered and looked around for a table. The room was crowded as usual and finding a table didn't look promising. Something caught Jenna's eye and she turned to see Hillary and Drake waving at them from their table. Jenna smiled and waved back. She and Adam weaved their way over to the table.

"Hi, Hillary, Drake," Jenna said to the couple.

"Well, if it isn't the mystery descrambler," Hillary smiled.

"'Descrambler'? Is that even a word?" Jenna asked. Hillary liked having a word of the week and 'descrambler' must be the one for this week.

"Doesn't matter. I like it."

"Join us," Drake said. "We have to leave soon to see a movie but we can visit for a while."

Jenna and Adam pulled out the extra chairs and sat. A server came over and they each ordered a drink, Adam a beer and Jenna an apple cider.

"Before I forget, I ordered those two books you wanted, Hillary. They should be in sometime this coming week."

"Good. I want to give one to a friend as a birthday present." She leaned on the table. "That sure was some engagement party last night. I haven't had so much fun in a long time. The decorations were beautiful, it was an excellent meal, and the speeches were short."

"And the music was perfect to dance to," Drake added.

Jenna waited while the server set two bottles and two glasses on the table. "Yes, we enjoyed ourselves too." As she poured the cider from the bottle into the glass Jenna tried to decide if she should tell Hillary and Drake about the note. It really wasn't much of a secret now that someone had apparently hacked Bill's Facebook account and put up the post. Plus, they might have seen something unusual that could still be fresh in their minds. "Did you get a request from Carla for your photos?"

"Yes, and I sent mine this afternoon."

Jenna took a deep breath and decided to bring Hillary and Drake into her confidence. "I was just about in bed last night when Carla phoned in a panic. Someone had left a note on the head table." Jenna dug out her phone and found the picture. She showed it to Hillary and Drake.

"'Bruce dump her or die'," Hillary read. "Really? Someone wrote that?"

"Yes, and left it under the rim of Bruce's plate."

"Why? Who would do that?" Drake asked.

"They don't know. No one at the head table saw who left it. Carla and Bruce told everyone at the table to keep quiet about it but early this morning a Facebook post was sent to them by Bill, one of the future groomsmen." Again, Jenna showed them the picture on her phone. "Apparently, there was a photo of them from last night with it. Carla and Bruce hid the post from their pages and contacted Bill. He claimed that he knew nothing about it and that he must have been hacked."

"Poor Carla and Bruce," Hillary sympathized. "What a way to end a happy evening. They must both be scared, what with her past."

"Yes, it's hard on them. Bruce is taking the note to the police but doesn't really expect that they can do much. Did either of you see anything unusual last night, someone acting strange?"

Hillary grinned. "I'm getting the impression you've been enlisted to help them."

"Pretty much. Adam is supposed to be my sidekick."

"Yeah, some sidekick I'm going to be. I was there and didn't see anything odd or curious."

Hillary shook her head. "I don't remember anything that I thought was strange. But since I didn't know any of the people there I wouldn't be a good observer."

"Same with me," Drake said.

"We should get going," Hillary said, standing. "The movie starts soon."

Drake also stood. He shook hands with Adam and leaned over to kiss Jenna's cheek.

"Thank you for the table," Adam said.

"Enjoy your movie," Jenna called as they left.

60

Adam signalled the waitress. "We'd like some potato skins and chicken fingers," he said. "And I'll have another beer."

"I still have some cider but I'd like some water please." Jenna had to drive. Adam usually took the bus after work but she would probably give him a ride home tonight. She frequently did when they went out for a relaxing drink after work.

The waitress came back immediately with the drinks. While they waited for the appetizers, Jenna forwarded the photos to Adam. They sipped on their drinks and studied each one making comments about who was in them, what was happening, and what part of the room was in the background.

"Nothing in the photos look promising," Adam said. "No one looks like they're skulking around the head table. No one looks like they have something to hide. No guilty expressions, no furtive looks. Everyone is enjoying themselves."

"Oh, that guy seems to have something to hide." Jenna handed her phone to Adam.

Adam looked at himself walking with a drink in his hand. "Oh, I don't know. I think he is the most handsome man there. And you can tell by his eyes that he is intelligent and honest."

Jenna laughed as she took her phone back. She liked spending time with Adam outside of work when the pressure of running a business was ended and they could unwind. He had a great sense of humour and always made her laugh.

The waitress came with their appetizers and set the plates on the table.

"Did Carla or Bruce say they noticed anything strange about any of the pictures?" Adam asked.

"Not so far." Jenna sighed. "I don't know why she thinks I can figure this out. But don't forget, according to Carla you're in on this too. And you were there last night. You might have seen something and just don't know it yet."

"The only people I knew were you, Hillary, Drake, and Carla and I've met Bruce once. I could have watched someone stand on their head and not know if that was normal behaviour or not."

"Well, I know Carla's sister and a few friends from when I worked for her. And from what I saw last night, you have a good chance of getting to know Bruce's side of the wedding party."

Adam blushed. "You mean Mason?"

"Yes. Are you going to meet up?"

"We did exchange phone numbers."

"And?"

"I'm not sure if I'm ready yet."

Jenna put her hand on his arm.

CHAPTER 8

"What do you think of meeting a man through a game?" Samantha asked.

"What do you mean?" Jenna frowned. It was Monday afternoon and she was meeting with one of her coaching clients. "Like at a football game?"

"No. Not quite. A month ago, I was invited by a friend to play *Scrabble* through an online app. I played two games with her and then I began getting new challenges from other players, people I didn't know. Their pictures showed up and at first I accepted a few because I liked playing. There's a little icon at the top left-hand corner that you can click on to send a message to, or receive a message from, your opponent.

"I wasn't interested in talking with them so I'd ignore it when it flashed with a message. Then people I was playing against began resigning from the games. I couldn't figure out why because neither one of us was winning or losing badly. One day I decided to see what one of the guys was messaging me. It was *Hello, how are you*? I checked another and there were four of them. *Hi. Hi. Where are you playing from? Why aren't you answering me?* I guess the ones I didn't answer got mad and resigned."

"That seems harmless," Jenna said, wondering where this was going. Samantha had been coming to her for a year in her quest to find the right guy. Jenna had spent hours coaching her on what to do on the first date, how to flirt a little on the second date, and how to decide if she wanted a third date. So far, all her coaching hadn't produced the type of relationship Samantha was looking for.

"It is but I decided to start answering some of them, especially the ones with cute pictures. One guy seems really nice and lives here in the city. He's asked me to meet for drinks. What do you think?"

"Well, that's a new one," Jenna said. She'd heard of people meeting at football or baseball games but never through an online *Scrabble* game. At outdoor sports events there was more opportunity to interact with someone new with other people around as buffers. "What else have you learned about him through your chats?"

"He's not married, he works as a bartender, and he has a dog."

"All things most men know a woman wants to hear," Jenna smiled. "No baggage, a good job, and he likes animals."

"Do you think he just said all that to make me think he was an upstanding guy?"

"I can't judge him but men have been known to stretch the truth a little to get a woman to go out with them."

Samantha sighed. "And just because he plays *Scrabble* doesn't mean he's honest and decent."

"You probably won't be able to find out the truth without going out with him."

"Where do you suggest we meet?"

"Since you don't have a profile on him to read, I would advise somewhere open with lots of people around. Preferably in the daylight."

"Okay." Samantha stood. "Thank you for your advice today. Maybe this will be the guy."

As she showed Samantha to the door, she saw Carla standing by the counter.

"Can I talk with you?" Carla asked.

Jenna looked at Adam behind the cash register. She felt guilty leaving him alone.

"It's okay," Adam said. "I can handle it."

Jenna led Carla back to her office. "What's happening?" she asked, when they were seated.

"Bruce went to the police yesterday. They took the information but they told him there was nothing they could do without more to go on. The constable said if anything else happens to let them know."

"Just as I figured. Any more photos?"

"A few but still nothing significant on them."

"What was the name of the catering company?" Jenna asked.

"The Distinctive Gourmet. Why?"

"How did you find them? Did someone recommend them?"

"Yes. A friend of my secretary used them for her daughter's wedding."

"So you hadn't met any of the owners or staff before?"

"No," Carla said, thoughtfully. "And therefore, I wouldn't know if all the ones dressed in uniforms were actually part of the staff."

"Would you be able to get the names of the employees who worked Saturday night?"

"I guess I could ask the manager. What reason should I give for wanting them if she's curious?"

"Um, tell her that you were so impressed with their work that you want to send them each a thank you card."

"Okay," Carla nodded.

Jenna was interested in Carla's relationship with Lillian. "What about the people at the head table?" Jenna asked. "Are you sure that none of them could have placed the note there?"

Carla hesitated. "No, I don't think so."

"You sure? How well do you know Bruce's groomsmen?"

"With Bruce going into business with Ronnie, I've gotten to know him. But I don't know Bill or Mason at all."

"Do you think Ronnie could have put the paper there, that he was trying to save his best friend from getting married?"

"He could have." Carla shrugged. "I think you should be asking Bruce these questions."

"I will but I just wanted to get your impressions of them. What about your bridesmaids?"

"What?" Carla stared at her.

"Do you think one of them might have done it?"

"No. Don't be silly. I've told you before, Monica is my sister, Lillian is my cousin, and I've known Rachael since middle school. I trust all of them."

"I noticed that you were abrupt with Lillian when she phoned you yesterday."

Carla sighed. "She can be clingy and pushy at the same time. I have to almost be mean to get my message across."

"Why did you invite her to be one of your bridesmaids?"

"Mom, Monica, and I are the only ones left in her family. She lives alone and doesn't have many friends. I guess I felt sorry for her more than anything. And I needed another bridesmaid because Bruce wanted a best man and two groomsmen."

Carla's phone pinged. She glanced at it. "It's more photos. I'll pass them on to you."

Jenna picked up her phone and both women scrolled through them. "Notice anything?" Jenna asked.

"No, but I'll go through them more carefully when I get home and I'll get Bruce to do the same." She put her phone in her purse and stood. "I have to go."

"Okay. Let me know what you learn from the caterer."

After Carla left, Jenna went to the counter. The store was empty and due to close in an hour and half.

"Why don't you leave early?" she said to Adam. "I'll get ready for the Monday ladies."

Two creative writing groups rented the back corner of the store for their meetings. Mondays were the Ladies' Creative Circle for Older Romance Writers. The All Writers' Troupe members were of all ages, all sexes, and wrote all genres and met once a month.

"Okay."

"Well, that was easy," Jenna grinned.

"Mason wants to meet for drinks."

"Oh, he works fast."

"I was surprised when he called, too."

"I'm glad for you."

"And yes, I will ask him about the note."

"That's my gumshoe detective buddy."

"I prefer the old-fashioned 'private dick'."

*J*enna got the coffee pot ready to be plugged in and took the cupcakes she'd bought earlier out of the fridge. Part of the services the ladies paid for was refreshments.

Jenna pushed the bookshelves on wheels to the side and set out chairs in a circle around a small coffee table. She placed napkins, paper cups and plates, plastic cutlery, and the cupcakes on the table.

The Loft staff opened its doors at ten o'clock and locked them at five-thirty. Each of the tenants had a key to one of the doors in case they wanted to get there early or stay late. The ladies were due to arrive at five-fifteen. Jenna plugged in the coffee pot and waited. The first was Amy, who had organized and ran the group. She was always early by about ten minutes.

Jenna and Amy discussed the weather and the Vancouver Canucks while waiting for the others. When they were all seated around the table at the back Jenna took the pot of coffee and set it down beside the cupcakes. That was the extent of her involvement. She retreated to the front.

Usually, Jenna was able to block out the conversation of the grey-haired women talking about the sex scenes they were writing for their steamy romance novels but tonight there seemed to be a lot of anger in their voices.

"Well, this is a review of my latest book *Love on a Stick*." There was a crackle of paper. *"In all honesty, I was only able to read half of this book. There is an amazing number of grammatical errors, the characters are one-dimensional, and I flinched at the dialogue. Don't authors proofread anymore? Only buy the book if you have nothing else to do with your time and your money."*

Her reading of the review was followed by comments of encouragement from the others.

"I read your book and I didn't find any errors and I loved the characters. I'll go in and mark it not helpful."

"That woman sounds like a real piece of work."

"You are a wonderful writer and the five-star reviews you get proves it. In my opinion, anyone who spouts this malice is jealous and is probably a failed writer."

"It really hurts when some spiteful person thinks she is a reviewer and trashes your baby. Don't let it get you down. Many other authors know and understand your pain."

"That's a good review compared to one I received," another woman said. "*This story is horrible. It was truly painful to read. The writing was way below par with peculiar phrasing and an undeveloped love story. The couple hardly had time together and then they were getting married. The romance is not believable. It's not worth the money or time.* I checked out the reviewer and found that she has downloaded eight romance books similar to mine and she has left a nasty review for each one. I feel like going in and outing her as a serial vicious reviewer."

"Maybe we should find out where this person lives and hire a hitman."

Jenna smiled at that statement. These ladies sure didn't sound like anyone's sweet grandma.

"I know it is frustrating to get these bad reviews but I'm not sure if a response from us as the authors will help the matter. They won't go away so we just have to keep on writing and ignore them."

At six, Jenna locked up, cashed out, and put the money in the safe. She returned to the counter and took out her cell phone. She began going through the photos Carla had sent again. She studied each one, sometimes enlarging them to check the looks on a certain face or to see what was in a person's hand. One photo had a catering staff member in it but the angle didn't allow her to see his face.

Her phone pinged. She looked at the text message from Drake wondering if she wanted to meet him somewhere for a drink. She explained about the ladies' writing group and said she could meet him about seven-thirty. She hung up then brought up Carla's photos again. She sighed. It didn't matter how many times she went through them, she couldn't find anything unusual. Finally she shook her head and decided to wait until she was with Carla and Bruce to look at them again.

When the ladies left just before seven o'clock, Jenna cleaned up the table, put the shelves back and locked up. She put on her coat and grabbed her umbrella from under the counter. She walked along the wet street to her car and drove to a restaurant on Cambie Street. The place was busy and it took a few moments for her to spot Drake waiting at a table. She shook off her umbrella and hurried over.

Drake stood. "Thank you for coming."

"Is something the matter?" Jenna took off her coat and sat down. She saw that he'd ordered her a coffee and a plate of nachos for them to share. She picked up a nacho with lots of cheese on it and popped it in her mouth.

Drake slid a piece of paper over to here. "I saw this on the news last night."

Jenna looked at the drawing of a black spider. Something niggled at her memory but didn't materialize. She looked questioningly at Drake.

"Apparently, the badly decomposed body of a man was found near the Fraser River. The police say there was no identification on him and they were unable to get any fingerprints but he had this tattoo. It seemed familiar to me and it took a while for me to remember where I'd seen it."

"Where?"

"Last spring two teenagers were at a party and overdosed. Their friends brought them to the emergency room. I administered Naloxone to the one who was my patient and he survived. His brother came in and was furious with him for being so stupid. Both brothers had a spider tattoo on their necks. It was like the one shown on the news."

"So, it looks like he may have overdosed again but this time didn't get help."

"Yes," Drake said, sadly.

Jenna put her hand on Drake's and squeezed. After his six-year-old nephew Jonathon's death ten years ago, Drake had turned to alcohol to deal with his pain and after a year, Jenna had broken up with him. Drake had eventually sobered up and gone to university to study medicine. He was now a doctor in the emergency ward where he could save the lives of accident, or overdose, or illness sufferers. He was always troubled when someone he attended ultimately died.

"I looked up his name in the hospital files and called the police with the information. The officer I talked with said it was a popular type of tattoo and they'd had quite a few phone calls about it already. He'd put the name and number on their list. I'm hoping it's not him or his brother."

"That's it." Jenna slapped the table excitedly. "I've seen that tattoo, also."

"Where?" Drake asked.

"At Jonathon's memorial." Jonathon had been killed by a hit-and-run driver while Drake was looking after him. The driver and passenger had gotten out of their vehicle while Drake was administrating CPR but when they saw how bad Jonathon was hurt they jumped back in their car and sped away. All Drake remembered about them was that they were young and smelled of alcohol. He hadn't gotten a license plate number and the police hadn't been unable to find the boys or the car. Jonathon's parents held an annual fundraising memorial fair, with a 5K run/walk, games for children to play, a couple of bouncy houses, and booths for businesses to sell their products, every spring on the anniversary of his death.

This past spring a man had approached Drake with the first name of his friend's brother who had been driving the car. Before he could give any more information he'd been scared off by something or someone. A little while later a man had snuck up behind Jenna and given her a piece of paper with a telephone number on it and told her to give it to Dr. Ferrell. Drake had called the number and arranged a meeting but the man never showed. This had happened before, someone contacting Drake or his brother claiming to have some information and wanting to meet somewhere but the address they gave turned out to be an empty lot or was even non-existent.

There was nothing they could do about those scammers and Drake had put the experience down to another person thinking it was funny to pretend to have information about a sensational story.

"Last spring at the fair. When that man was hurrying away after giving me the note for you I saw something on his neck that didn't quite register at the time. Now I realize it was a spider tattoo like this one."

"Really?" Drake asked eagerly. "You saw it on his neck?"

"Yes," Jenna said. "I wonder if the body is of the man who was supposed to meet you. Did the police say where on the man's body the tattoo was?"

"No. But if the spider looks the same, it could mean the reason he didn't show up to our meeting was because he was dead."

"It might not be him," Jenna pointed out. She knew how much his nephew's death still haunted Drake and she didn't want him to be disappointed again.

The plate of nachos was finished and Drake signaled for the bill. "I'm going back to the hospital and get the phone number I gave the police. Maybe someone at that number knows something."

"Thank you for the snack," Jenna said as Drake walked her to her car. "Let me know if you learn anything."

"I'm so glad I have you to talk to." Drake gave her a hug.

Jenna drove to her condo. She really hoped that Drake would find closure sometime soon.

Early the next morning Jenna's phone rang. She'd been expecting the call.

"Hi, Drake."

"I called the phone number I had for the man with the tattoo and talked with his mother, Mrs. Hiscock. I explained everything to her and she told me the police had phoned her but she didn't believe the man was either of her sons. She also said neither of them had anything to do with Jonathon's death and she hung up."

"Oh, that's too bad." Another dead end for Drake.

"I'm not going to give up. I'll find the boys, or men now, who did it, yet. I won't give up."

"I'm here to help you," Jenna said.

"I know. Thank you."

CHAPTER 9

*A*dam walked into the Earl's Kitchen and Bar and looked around. He saw Mason sitting at a corner table. Mason smiled and waved and half stood when Adam approached. He was wearing black jeans, a white sweater, and a black vest. The server came over to leave menus and take their drink orders.

"We have some wonderful craft beer," the server said.

"Beer is so common." Mason shook his head. "What do you put in your Moscow Mule Mimosa?"

"One third orange juice, one third ginger beer and one third champagne."

"I'll take a glass, please."

"That sounds good," Adam said. "I'd like one, also."

"Do you want to order an appetizer?" Mason asked, opening his menu.

"Okay." Adam looked through the appetizer section. "The honey and garlic wings and the bruschetta look good."

"So does the hummus and pita."

"Let's do all three."

"This looks like the bar where they used to film the show *First Dates*," Adam said, after the server came back with their drinks and they'd placed their order. He wasn't sure how much small talk they should do before he brought up the subject of the piece of paper left on the head table. Besides exchanging phone numbers in the short time they'd talked at the party, they'd told each other where they lived, and that they were both single.

"No, that's Earl's in Yaletown," Mason said. "I was on that show on the first season, but not as one of the three dates filmed. My date and I were part of the background."

"And how did that work out?" Adam took a sip of his drink. It had an unusual flavour that he liked. He was glad Mason had asked for it.

"Not very good. We didn't match. So why are you still single? How come you've never been swept up?"

"I was in a relationship but he left."

"Left, as in …"

"One day he decided he wanted to go back to his ex." Adam didn't want to say any more than he had to. It was still a difficult subject.

"Oh, I'm so sorry."

The server returned with two plates and cutlery wrapped in a cloth napkin. He left them in the centre of the table.

"What about you?" Adam asked, as he took a plate and cutlery. "Any serious relationships?"

"Not lately."

"How long was your longest relationship?"

"Well." Mason began laughing.

"Oh," Adam grinned. "You're going to say a month, two months."

"Um, four months."

"You don't stick around long."

"I'm a flight attendant and it's sometimes hard to maintain a bond with just one person."

"So you have a man in every airport?" Adam wondered if Mason would get the joke based on sailors supposedly having a girl in every port.

"Oh, you are sharp," Mason said. "And what do you do?"

"I co-own a bookstore." This might be a good way of getting to the note. "My business partner, Jenna Hamilton, is a friend of Carla's. I was her plus-one."

"How lucky for both of us."

"Yes. And Carla phoned Jenna when they found the note."

"So, you know about that."

"Yes. Carla asked Jenna and me to look into who might have left it."

"Why you two? Why not the police?"

"The police don't have anything to go on and Jenna figured out what happened in the death of a friend last spring."

"Oh." Mason was quiet. "Is that why you agreed to meet me, to find out what I know?"

Adam had a few minutes to think as the server arrived with their plates of appetizers. Mason moved his glass so the plates could be lined up in front of them. He cocked his head at Adam.

"No—well, yes. I'd already accepted your invite and then Jenna asked me to mention the note." It was a little lie but Adam felt it was necessary this time. He took a couple of wings and a bruschetta so he didn't have to look Mason in the eye. He wasn't good at lying.

"I don't know anything. I never saw anyone leave the note. Is that good enough?"

"Look, I didn't mean to make you mad. Jenna is just trying to help a friend and I agreed to find out what I could that might be of assistance."

"Sorry." Mason waved his hand. "I can't understand why anyone would do it, especially since Carla has lost two fiancés already."

"I know. That's why she asked Jenna to help. She doesn't know what else to do."

"Okay, what do you want to ask me?"

Adam didn't have a clue. Jenna made soliciting information look so easy and she always seemed to know what to ask. "As Bruce's cousin, do you know of anyone who might have a grudge against him?"

"As in someone who wanted to ruin his evening?" Mason spooned some hummus onto his plate and took a couple of pieces of pita bread.

"Or someone who wanted to scare him into cancelling his engagement?"

"Like an old girlfriend?"

"Yes."

"Well, he did break up with Ronnie's cousin, Linda, just after he met Carla."

"Would she still be mad about that?" Adam bit into the bruschetta. Delicious.

"I don't even know if she was mad at the time. It didn't take her long to find another guy."

"What about a business deal that went wrong or someone he fired?" Adam was glad he occasionally watched *Homicide Hunter*.

"Nothing that I've heard of."

"Does he have any financial problems?" Sometimes people married someone rich to get themselves out of money difficulties.

"Not as far as I know."

"What type of business does he have?"

"He owns three craft beer breweries."

"Where are they situated?" Adam looked at the wings on his plates. Wasn't one of the rules on the show, *First Dates,* was that you weren't supposed to order anything messy? He picked up his knife and fork and pulled at the meat on the bones.

"Two are in Vancouver and one in Squamish."

"Is there anything you can tell me that might explain who sent the note and why?"

Mason hesitated.

"What?"

"Well, I said Linda had found a new guy shortly after she and Bruce split up but there's more to it."

"What?" Adam asked again.

"The only reason I'm telling you is because of the threat to Bruce. You have to promise not to tell Carla."

Adam didn't know what Jenna would do in this situation but if he wanted this information, he'd have to agree. And it might be important. "I promise."

"And I know you'll tell Jenna, so you have to swear she doesn't tell Carla."

"I really can't speak for her."

"I can't tell you without that agreement."

"Okay, I'll tell her not to say anything." He hoped Jenna would go along with it.

"Well, two weeks ago Bruce and Linda hooked up for a few nights."

"Oh." Adam sat back in his chair. According to Joe Kenda on *Homicide Hunter*, the three main reasons for a person to kill someone else are sex, money, and revenge. Linda could have two of those reasons. "So she could be a little resentful."

"Knowing Linda, I don't think so. She didn't even try to speak with Bruce at the party."

"She was at the party?" Adam stared at Mason. "Why would Bruce invite her?"

"He didn't. Ronnie did. She was his plus-one."

Adam didn't know what to say to that. "Wasn't that a bit odd? Why would he do that?"

Mason shrugged. "Maybe he just needed to get back at him."

"What for?"

"You'll have to ask them."

Adam was out of questions. He hoped he'd covered all the topics Jenna had wanted. Now he could relax and really get to know Mason. Hopefully, Mason still wanted to know him better.

CHAPTER 10

"**B**ruce did what?" Jenna stared at Adam, her mouth open. They were standing behind the counter, waiting until ten o'clock to open their store.

"Had a few nights' stand with an old girlfriend."

Jenna closed her mouth and tried to absorb the news. "After he was engaged to Carla?"

"Yes, two weeks ago."

"Oh. My. God." Jenna couldn't believe it. She'd promised not to tell Carla what she was going to hear, but now that she knew what that agreement involved, how could she not tell her? She looked at Adam. "What do I do now?"

"For sure don't tell Carla," Adam warned. "I promised Mason. And ..." He paused as if for dramatic effect.

"What?"

"She was at the party as Ronnie's plus-one."

"She was?" Jenna gaped at him in disbelief. "Why would Ronnie do that?"

"Mason said Ronnie did it to get back at Bruce for something but he wouldn't tell me what. It seems strange that as a long-time friend, he would flaunt Bruce's infidelity at his own engagement party."

"Bruce told me none of his exes were at the party," Jenna said, then shook her head. "No, wait. He said he hadn't invited any of his exes."

"I guess, technically, he hadn't."

Jenna nodded. "Right. And now we know why he never said anything about her. I wonder what else he lied to us or misled us about."

"We may have to talk with him privately to find out."

"How did you get Mason to tell you about it?"

"He was quite forthcoming with it, almost as if he enjoyed telling me."

"Strange." She needed time to think about the news she'd just heard and decide how to deal with it. "Did you learn anything that might help us?"

"Well, Bruce owns three craft beer breweries. The business deal Ronnie spoke about in his speech is that he and Bruce are going to set up one in Whistler together. It doesn't sound as if Bruce has any financial problems, so he isn't after Carla for her money. Mason can't think of anyone from Bruce's past who would want to harm him. I couldn't come up with anything else to ask."

Jenna smiled. "You did well. You found out more than I expected. And in your sleuthing, did you have time to learn anything about Mason?"

"He's a flight attendant, he's got a younger sister who he doesn't want to talk about, and he doesn't like beer. He says it's too common."

"An odd way of putting it."

"And he doesn't stay in relationships very long."

"Oh. That doesn't sound very promising."

"I thought that too, but then I'm not sure if I'm ready for a serious relationship. Just having a friend to go out with once in a while is good for now."

"Are you going to see him again?"

"I'd like to. He's flying out today and won't be back in the city until the weekend. He's going to call when he returns."

Jenna looked at the clock. Time to open the shop. She went around the end of the counter and headed to the door while Adam shook the cat treat tin. She moved to avoid being hit by

Trish dashing around one of the shelves and bent to pet Maggie as she ambled over for her treats. She unlocked the door.

"Do you want to get out the decorations or should I?" Jenna asked Adam when she was back at the counter. It was the first week of October and time to decorate for Hallowe'en.

"I'll get them."

"Okay." Jenna went out the door into the hallway and looked at their large display window. New releases and best sellers were displayed along with a sample of the used books, magazines, novelties, and ornaments they also sold. They didn't have many Hallowe'en decorations but each year they tried to decorate the window differently and add something new and unique to attract the attention of shoppers.

Jenna went back inside the store as Adam plunked two boxes on the counter. These were from past years. Jenna reached under the counter for the bag of new decorations she'd purchased the week before. She set it beside the others, as a couple entered. Jenna smiled at them.

"Do you have any books on weddings?" the woman asked.

There wasn't much call for wedding books anymore. Wedding planners and apps now took up a large part of the industry. But some prospective brides, Carla included, still wanted to look at the pictures and read the write-ups in one spot as opposed to scrolling from one site to another trying to decide. Jenna had ordered a few books besides the one Carla had asked for.

"We do have some new ones and a few in our used-book section," Adam said. "I'll show you." He led them towards the back.

Jenna's mind turned to her dilemma as she sorted through the Hallowe'en decorations. What should she do with the news she'd heard about Bruce? There were supporters for both sides of what to do if you learn the spouse or partner of a friend is having an affair: tell them or not tell them. Jenna personally would want to know so that she didn't waste any more of her life on a man who didn't love and respect her enough to be faithful. But she knew there were others who thought it was better to remain in the dark because they didn't want to end their marriage, whether it was because they truly loved the person or because they didn't want to be alone.

It came down to what she thought Carla would want. And that, she didn't know.

Jenna carried some of the decorations to the window. She moved the books and novelties aside. In their place, she set two orange and black cushions with ghosts and bats stitched on them, three large black spiders, and a black bowl full of small, orange artificial pumpkins. She picked Maggie and her cushion off her wooden chair by the door and used the chair to stand on to hang two strings of dangling bats, pumpkins, spiders, ghosts, and skeletons from the ceiling. She put the books and novelties throughout the decorations then went out into the hallway again to view her work.

"Forgot something," she muttered, and went back inside. One of the new things she had purchased was a plaque. She found it in the bag and placed it in one corner of the window. She went back out and smiled as she read it: *If you are reading this, then you are blissfully unaware of what is creeping up behind you.* She hoped it might make some people glance over their shoulders.

Adam was ringing up a sale for two books, a brightly-coloured vase, and a set of four hand-painted coasters for the couple as Jenna set the *Happy Hallowe'en* mat with orange pumpkins in front of the door. Using Maggie's chair again, she thumb tacked long flowing ghosts and large, black witches' hats to the ceiling over the bookshelves. Jenna replaced Maggie's chair by the door and set the cushion back on it.

"It's all yours," Jenna said, to the cat waiting by the door.

Maggie jumped up on it and settled down. Jenna patted Maggie then went to the office. There was a permanent umbrella stand by the door for people to leave their damp umbrellas as they entered. Last week she'd confiscated her friends' corn brooms and she now gathered them up and carried them to the front. Jenna placed the brooms in the stand, handle, or bar as she'd learned it was called, down and their heads in the air. It looked like a number of witches had parked their modes of transportation while shopping.

Jenna surveyed her handiwork. She'd seen pictures of houses that had huge spider webs running from the top of the roof to the front sidewalk and a gigantic spider going up and down the web. She wished she could do something similar in the shop, but there just wasn't room.

"Looks good," Adam said.

"Thank you." Jenna smiled at him. "Next year is your turn."

"Have you decided what you are going to do about Bruce?"

"No." Jenna joined him behind the counter. "I've been trying to figure that out all morning. Did Mason say we couldn't tell Bruce we know about the affair?"

"No. He just didn't want Carla to find out and the only reason he told me about it is because he's worried about the threat to Bruce."

"I think one of us has to speak with Bruce."

"It can't be me. I've only met him once and I was at the party because of you. That isn't a subject I could just walk up to him and start talking about."

"Yeah, you're right." Jenna bit her lip. "But how do I bring it up?"

The bell jingled and two women walked in, laughing. "That's a cute sign you have in the window," one of them said.

"Yes, it made me check over my shoulder," the other said, as they headed to the used-book section.

*T*uesday morning, Carla stared at a picture on her cell phone. It had been sent to her by Monica, who had also added a text that she wondered if this was the person who could have left the note. The photo was blurry, as if the person taking it was dancing or had had too much to drink or had tripped. It showed a group of people standing near the table talking. In the lower right corner a woman leaned over the head table. The picture was taken from behind and only half of her was in view. Carla enlarged it as much as she could but that only made it fuzzier.

"Damn," Carla said. She could see that the colour of her outfit was light blue but couldn't make out her hairstyle. She looked at the other people in the photo. Was that her secretary, Sandra, and her husband talking with one of her suppliers? She couldn't be sure. She tossed the phone on the coffee table in frustration.

Carla stood and walked to the window. She looked out over Burrard Inlet below her. She should be at work but had cancelled her appointments for the week. There was no way she would be able to concentrate after getting that message. She went back to the coffee table and picked up her phone. She tapped in her sister's number and put it on speaker.

"Hi, Monica. I've studied the photo you sent and I can't make out who the woman might be."

"I had the same trouble. Kevin took it and he apologized for the quality of it. He'd forgotten that I'd asked him to take some photos on my cell and when he remembered near the end of the evening, he just stood up and started snapping pictures. By then he was a little unsteady on his feet. He doesn't really remember taking that particular one and of course he wouldn't know who she was if he did."

"How many others do you have?" Carla asked.

"About ten. I looked through them and didn't see anyone else close to the table or another one of her."

"Can you send them to me anyway?"

"Sure. I'll do that as soon as we hang up. And while I have you on the phone, are you and Bruce still coming to my opening night tonight?"

"Oh."

"You've forgotten," Monica chided.

"I'm sorry. I haven't been able to think about anything else except the note."

"That's okay. It's just that, as one of the backers of the play, you should be there."

"I know." After becoming a certified dental assistant, Monica had joined the Alliance Theatre Dramatic Society. She'd started out on the set-building crew, progressed to wardrobe, and then to parts in the plays. She tried to perform in one play a year. Carla attended Monica's shows and this year had come on board as a producer, which was just a fancy name for someone who put up some of the money to fund the play. She'd watched a couple of rehearsals and saw how the actors and actresses came together as a group as they learned their lines and blocking. She'd even gone backstage and observed the pieces of the set being built. Monica wanted her to try out for a role but getting up in front of a theatre full of people was not on her bucket list.

"Carla?"

"Sorry, I was just thinking."

"About what?"

"About how glad I am that you do what you do. Watching you and the other actors pull together to get a play from paper to the stage is impressive."

"Thank you. I really enjoy it and it is a total departure from my real job. It gives some excitement to my life."

"And stress and an ulcer," Carla laughed, recalling Monica talking about the times when actors arrived late, or sets fell apart, or someone got sick. "But yes, I will be there. I don't know about Bruce. He's meeting with a construction company to discuss the new building in Whistler."

"Well, there are two seats reserved under your name, so bring someone else if you wish."

"Will do."

After she hung up, Carla phoned Jenna. There was no use reminding Bruce of the opening night. If he did get out of the meeting early, he'd just want to relax at home with more paperwork. She remembered their first few dates when their evenings had been interrupted by phone calls from investors and employees and real estate agents. When the site had been chosen and land bought and the architect had the blueprints drawn and the best bid from a construction company selected, his life had settled down a bit and they'd enjoyed their time together. But now that construction was about to begin, the tension had increased.

Carla knew about franchises but from the other side. She sold franchises of her business whereas Bruce bought his.

"Hello, Carla," Jenna said.

"Jenna. I have a photo that shows a woman bending over the head table but the quality is terrible and I can't make out who she is."

"Oh, that's too bad."

"Yes, I've tried enlarging it but it just gets worse. I'll send it to you along with the others my sister sends me."

"Does she remember taking the picture and who that woman might be?

"Her fiancé took it and he doesn't know who she is."

"Oh. It would have been nice to find the person so quickly."

"It sure would. But I called you on another matter also. Are you free tonight?"

"Yes, after we close at six."

"How would you like to go see my sister perform in a play at the Alliance Theatre as my guest?"

"Oh, I would love to. What time should I meet you?"

"It starts at seven-thirty and I usually get there half an hour early."

"Okay, see you there at seven o'clock."

CHAPTER 11

Jenna hung up the phone. It was good to hear from Carla. Other than sending the photos, Carla had been mainly silent and Jenna had thought that she was on her own with this mystery. But Carla sounded normal on the phone, so maybe she was wrong.

Jenna grinned at Adam. "Guess who is going to the Alliance Theatre for the opening night of a play tonight?"

"Well, I know it's not me. Who invited you?"

"Carla. Her sister Monica is an actress and is in a new stage play there."

"Oh, a talented woman."

"It appears so. I've only met her a few times. She's a dental assistant by day."

"What is the play about?"

"Carla didn't say. But I don't care," Jenna smiled. "It's a free night out. Plus, Carla said she has a picture of a woman leaning over the head table but she can't make out much about her."

Jenna's phone pinged. She looked at it and saw that Carla had sent the pictures. She scrolled through them and found the one Carla had told her about. It was blurry as Carla had said. She held the phone so Adam could see it.

He shook his head. "Too bad you can't see who she is."

"Yes, but maybe if we show it to some of the people who were there someone might know her or remember seeing her. I'll discuss it with Carla tonight."

"Isn't today your blog day?" Adam asked.

Jenna looked around the store. There were only the two women who were now over at the romance section. "I won't be long."

Jenna went to the office and brought up her notes on the computer. She had a website advertising her dating coach business and a blog where she discussed the many phases of dating. Today she wanted to write about how to do some lighthearted flirting:

>*Your first date should be kept light and spent getting to know the person, finding out if you like that person, and deciding if you want to see that person again. If you enjoy your first date and choose to go on a second date, you can begin a little flirting. Flirting is a learned skill like riding a bicycle. You can compliment them on their clothes. But instead of saying 'That's a pretty blouse or that's a nice tie' say 'That blouse brings out the colour of your eyes' or 'you look great in the tie'.*

>*On your second date, if you are walking or sitting close enough, fleetingly rest your hand on his or her arm to show you are listening and liking the conversation. Stay relaxed and don't try to have too profound a discussion. As on your first date, keep it simple by asking questions about what types of movies they like or how often they've moved in their life. And remember something from the first date, like the name of their first pet as a child if it was mentioned.*

>*If you are at a party or in a bar and want to meet someone, you could walk past them and look them in the eye and smile. Or you could buy them a drink and have it sent to them. Their reaction will let you know if they are interested. At one time, a light brush against someone in a crowded room could be part of flirting but now, with unwanted touching being considered*

offensive, the idea has gone by the wayside. Keep your hands and body to yourself until you know the person better.

Jenna read over what she had written, tweaked it a bit, and posted it to her blog. She checked to see if there were any more questions or comments about her previous post and answered two. They were hosting a book reading and signing next week, so she printed the flyer she'd designed when she and the author had agreed on a date. She went into the bookstore again and showed the flyers to Adam.

"Nice," he said. "You should get into graphic designing."

"No, thanks," Jenna laughed. "I have enough to keep me busy." She looked around the store. There were a few customers wandering the aisles between the shelves. Nothing she couldn't handle.

"Time for your lunch break," Jenna said, walking behind the counter.

"Good, I'm starved." Adam patted Maggie on her head as he went out the door.

On their busy days, one of them would go to the café in the Net Loft or run across to the Public Market and grab something for both of them from one of the food stalls. On their less demanding days, they would each take a half hour lunch in order to get out of the store for a while.

Jenna rang up a sale of three books and a two-piece decorative box set, and another of two children's books and a set of six infinity stones. A UPS driver entered the store with a box. He was tall with dark hair and a ready smile.

"Good morning," Jenna smiled back. "You're new."

"To this route." He set the box on the counter. "I've been delivering for three years."

"Well, welcome to Granville Island." Jenna signed the machine and handed it back to him.

"Thank you." He touched his hat and left.

"That was short and sweet," Jenna murmured. The last driver, Tom, usually stopped and chatted a bit, updating her on his nine-year-old daughter who was into golf and his infant son who was just learning to walk.

Jenna opened the box and took out the books she'd ordered for the reading and signing, plus some others for customers. She reached under the counter and brought up the display box. She put a flyer in the box then arranged a couple of the books in front of it so the information could be seen. She took the rest of the books for the reading to the fantasy section, where she placed them prominently on the top shelf. She taped one of the flyers just below them.

The old school bell on the counter dinged. Jenna hurried to the counter and smiled at the man standing with two books in his hand.

"Did you find everything you were looking for?"

"Well, not exactly. I was hoping to find the book *Ninth House*."

"Ah." Jenna thought back. "We don't have a new copy. There might be one in the used-book section. Did you check there?"

"Yes. I didn't see one."

"Would you like me to order one for you? It could be here next week."

"Okay."

Jenna took down his name and phone number and promised to call him when it came in. She then packed up the two books he did buy.

Adam entered the store as she was taping one of the reading and book signing flyers at eye level on the door. Her stomach rumbled.

"Was that a greeting or a hint?"

"A bit of both," Jenna laughed.

"Then off you go."

"I'll put one flyer on the display board here in the Loft and take one for the board in the Public Market."

*J*enna hurried home after they closed the store and ate the sandwich she'd purchased with her lunch. She changed into a skirt and blouse, put on her cashmere coat, and slung her small gold purse over her shoulder. She went outside to wait for the taxi she'd booked before leaving the store. At the Alliance Theatre, she paid the driver and walked over to Carla who was standing under the marquee. She had on a black knee-length coat and black boots. They entered the theatre together and each was given a program. The foyer was crowded as people mingled with glasses in their hands. The two sets of double doors into the house were open and a few attendees were trickling through them to their seats.

"Would you like a drink?" Jenna asked.

"A glass of wine would be nice," Carla said.

"I'll be right back." Jenna got in line at the bar and asked for two glasses of red wine. She paid for them and carried them to where Carla waited by one of the bar style tables. Jenna set Carla's glass on the table and took a sip of her own.

Carla passed her cell phone to Jenna. "What did you think of the picture I sent?"

Jenna looked at the blurry photo. It didn't look any better on Carla's phone than it had on hers. "I don't know what to think. It's not that good. What colour do you think her dress is?"

"It looks light blue to me."

Jenna nodded. "Who are these other people?"

"I think it's my secretary and her husband and one of my suppliers. I didn't go to my office yesterday or today, so I haven't shown it to Sandra."

That didn't sound like Carla and Jenna was a little surprised. Carla was always on top of what was occurring and in the face of obstacles, she made things happen. Jenna felt sorry for her. Carla was a lovely woman who deserved happiness and Jenna had thought that this time she had found it.

"Would you be able to send it to her?" Jenna asked gently. She didn't want to make it sound like she was pushing.

Carla grinned. "You don't have to pussyfoot around me. I finally snapped out of my pity party this afternoon. I did that before I came here. I haven't heard back from her, yet."

"Were you able to get the names of the employees of Distinctive Gourmet?" Might as well keep the ball rolling.

"The manager will send it to me tomorrow."

"So she believed you about the cards."

"I've always been a good persuader." Carla grinned.

"Maybe we should go in." Jenna noticed the room was emptying as everyone headed to the doors.

They left their empty glasses and Jenna followed Carla to the door. Carla handed their tickets to the usher and they went to their seats. The house was three-quarters full and a heavy, red-velvet curtain was drawn across the stage. Jenna thumbed through the program. There were headshots of everyone involved in the play. Monica was listed as one of the actresses. The doors closed and the lights dimmed. Jenna closed her program. An announcer stepped through the opening in the curtain panels and welcomed everyone. He gave the ground rules: no pictures, if you leave you will not be allowed back until the end of the act, no talking, no heckling or booing, and no smoking.

"The two acts are approximately forty-five minutes each," he finished. "Enjoy your evening."

It had been a long time since she'd been to a play, so Jenna sat back to do exactly what the announcer advised. The play was a comedy from the 1950s and it didn't disappoint. There was a lot of laughter throughout the crowd. One of the actors seemed vaguely familiar. Was he the man who had stood and waved when Monica introduced her fiancé at Carla and Bruce's engagement party? Was he Kevin?

Jenna discreetly opened her program but the light from the stage didn't reach far enough for her to see it. Then she decided to relax. She would find out at intermission.

When the first act ended and the lights went up, Jenna blinked at the brightness. "Should we get up and stretch our legs?" she asked Carla.

"Yes."

They stood and slowly followed the others in their row to the aisle and joined the horde working their way to the open doors.

Some headed to the lines at the bar, some went outside for a smoke, and others just found a place to stand.

Jenna and Carla leaned against the wall. Jenna looked through her program and found a headshot of a man with a receding hairline. The name underneath was Kevin Barkley. She held the picture to Carla. "Is that Monica's fiancé?"

"Yes."

"I thought I recognized him. It must be nice for the two of them to work together."

"That's how they met. He tried out for a role in the play this year and they started dating during rehearsals. They got engaged shortly before Bruce and I did."

"And now you two are going to have a double wedding." Jenna immediately wished she could take back that statement when she saw the crestfallen look on Carla's face. "I'm sorry. I guess that's all put on hold under the circumstances."

"Well, we haven't officially called off our engagement, but I wouldn't be surprised if Bruce backed out. In fact, I've told him I'd understand if he did."

"And what did he say?"

"So far, he's sticking it out but we don't talk as much as we used to."

Jenna thought of Linda, Bruce's former love interest. Was he going back to her?

"Jenna?"

"Oh, I'm sorry." Jenna tried to block thoughts of Bruce and his former girlfriend and concentrate on what Carla was saying.

"Bruce claims he and Ronnie have meetings with Whistler city officials and the construction company head guys but I'm not so sure."

Neither was Jenna.

The second act was about to start and everyone filed back in. Jenna laughed throughout the remainder of the play. The curtains closed as the audience applauded its appreciation. When the curtain reopened, the players were lined up in a row. They all held hands and bowed. A few flowers were thrown up ontofor most of the stage. The announcer stepped out and introduced each of the actors and actresses. As their name was called, they each took another bow or did a curtsy and left the stage.

"I want to thank you so much for coming to opening night. If you enjoyed yourselves, please tell your family and friends. Goodnight." The announcer waved as the curtain closed in front of him.

"Monica invited us to come backstage," Carla said, as they made their way up the aisle to the foyer. "Do you want to go?"

"Oh, could I?" Jenna had always heard how prestigious it was to be invited backstage, that it was the ultimate experience to meet the actors of a play or, if at a concert, to meet the band members.

"Sure, come with me."

Carla led Jenna to a set of stairs with a velvet rope across the top. She unclipped one end and they both stepped down. She re-clipped it behind her.

"It's not really backstage," Carla laughed. "It's more like downstairs."

They walked down a narrow hallway past washrooms and a room full of costumes to a set of two doors, one on each side of the hall. *Men's Dressing Room* was on a plaque on one while *Women's Dressing Room* was on the other. Carla knocked on the women's doors. It was opened by Monica who was still in her costume.

"I was hoping you would come back here," she smiled, holding the door for them to enter.

Jenna looked around the long room. Dresses and skirts from the 1950s hung on a rack in one corner or from hooks on the walls. Five women chatted as they sat on chairs in front of a lengthy mirror and removed their make-up or wandered in various stages of undress. One grabbed her street clothes and went behind a screen to change.

"Hey, ladies," Monica said. "Most of you know my sister, Carla, and this is her friend, Jenna. I invited them to come back after the show."

Some of them waved, some said hi.

"Not very glamorous," Monica laughed. "And it gets hectic when we are all trying to dress at the same time before the play. That's why I wait for some of them to leave before I start changing after the evening is over."

"Doesn't that mean you walk to your car alone?" Jenna asked. It wasn't always safe for a woman at night.

"Oh, I park on the street," Monica said. "It's more expensive but better lit than the parking lot."

"See you all tomorrow night," one woman called to the others, as she brushed past Jenna and Carla on her way out the door.

"Well, we should leave," Carla said. "We don't want to be in the way."

"Thank you for coming," Monica said.

Jenna followed Carla up the stairs and out the front door onto the sidewalk. Some members of the audience were still hailing cabs or visiting.

"Would you like to go for a snack and a drink?" Jenna asked. The sandwich had disappeared hours ago and she was hungry.

"I'll take a rain check on that," Carla said. "I'm starting to get a headache."

"Oh, I'm sorry to hear that. I'll get you a cab." Jenna waved her hand but it took three tries before a passing taxi stopped. She opened the door for Carla. "Thank you for the invite to the play. I haven't laughed so much in a long time. Your sister is very talented."

"Thank you for coming with me. I needed an evening out." Carla smiled as she slid into the vehicle. "Tomorrow we get busy at finding out who sent that note and why."

"Good." Jenna shut the door and watched the taxi drive away. She hated knowing a devastating secret that had the potential of shattering her friend's very soul. Carla loved Bruce and really wanted to marry him. Jenna didn't want to destroy her happiness.

CHAPTER 12

*C*arla rubbed her temples in the back of the cab. Being hungry or tired were the two main reasons she ever got a headache. She'd eaten before going to the theatre and she'd had a nap to catch up on the sleep she'd missed the last two nights. It might have something to do with the slight change in Jenna's demeanour during the intermission when they talked about Bruce. She'd sensed Jenna knew something she wasn't telling her. She'd been about to ask her when they'd been called back into the house. She hadn't been able to concentrate on the rest of the play and had been glad when the lights went up even though the brightness had hurt her head.

Carla thought about not going backstage but knew her sister would be disappointed. So she and Jenna had made a quick appearance then left. Her head was pounding by then and she only wanted to get home. The taxi pulled up in front of her condo building. Carla paid and went inside. She nodded at a couple who were leaving. They lived on the floor below her. In her condo, Carla turned on her cell phone and saw a text message from her mother and a voicemail from Bruce. She looked at the clock and decided her mother would still be up. She dialed her number.

"Hi, Mom."

"Carla, thank you for calling me back. I have some news about Roberta and Conrad."

"Oh? What?" Carla put her phone on speaker and walked through her bedroom into the ensuite. She set it on the counter and rummaged through the cabinet.

"Well, I thought about what you'd said and I looked up the last landline number I had for them and I called it. I was surprised when Conrad answered."

"So they still live in the same place." Carla popped two painkillers into her mouth and washed them down with a glass of water.

"Yes. He wasn't happy when I identified myself but I convinced him to talk with me."

"Talk or yell?" Carla returned to her bedroom.

"He actually talked rationally."

"That's unusual." Carla remembered the times he and his mother had unexpectedly shown up when she, her mother, and sister were leaving a restaurant or taking a walk in a park and had start yelling and threatening them.

"Yes, I agree. I asked him if he and his mother had been at the engagement dinner and he said no."

Carla doubted that he would have admitted crashing the party. She removed her slacks and sweater and put on her housecoat.

"In fact, he said they didn't even know you were engaged again."

"Well, it's only been a three weeks."

"He added we didn't have to worry about them bothering us anymore."

"Or any less?" Carla tried to joke. It didn't work. She walked into her living room. "Do you believe him?"

"I don't know. His voice had his usual smarmy, oily intonation to it and I could almost see him rubbing his hands in glee like on the cartoons when one of the characters is up to something."

"Did he say why they are finally going to leave us alone?"

"I asked him and he said we have someone else to worry about."

"Else?" Carla asked in bewilderment. "What did he mean by that? Who could that be?"

"All he said was, 'You'll see.'"

"You'll see?" Carla felt a jolt of fear. "That sounds scary."

"That's what I thought. I asked him what he meant and he just emitted a nasty laugh and hung up."

This wasn't good. "I don't trust them. I wonder what they're up to and who this someone else is."

"Yes, me too. It seems strange that they decided to back off at the same time Bruce is threatened."

"They're up to something. Be careful, Mom, and don't let them into your place. Actually, don't let anyone you don't know into your place. Call the police if you have to."

"And you watch out, too. You know they dislike you and Monica as much as they dislike me."

"Have you told Monica about the phone call?"

"I left her a message also. I knew both of you were busy with her play opening tonight."

Carla pressed the end button and set her phone on the counter. What had Conrad meant that they had to worry about someone else coming at them? Did that mysterious person have something to do with the note left on the head table? Was it someone she knew? Was that why she hadn't noticed a stranger at the party?

In spite of the painkillers, her headache was worsening. She knew it was because of the stress she was under right now. She had to go back to her office tomorrow. Maybe signing papers and making deals and holding meetings would take her mind off what was happening in her private life.

$\mathcal{T}$he bell over the door jingled and Adam looked up to see Carla enter. She seemed agitated and distracted and walked right past Maggie who gave her a dirty look.

"Can I talk with you both?" Carla asked, striding up to the counter.

"Sure!" Jenna said. "We usually don't have any customers this early so we can stay here at the counter.

"I'll get you a chair," Adam said. He went to the children's story-telling section and brought back one of the adult chairs.

Adam and Jenna perched on the stools while Carla sat on the chair.

"What's the matter?" Jenna asked.

Carla took a deep breath and let it out. "There are two people in my past I should tell you about."

Adam saw Jenna's look of surprise and his first thought was why hadn't Carla mentioned this before?

"Oh?" Jenna raised her eyebrow. "Who?"

"My step-father, Hayden, was married before. His ex-wife and son have harassed mom and Monica and me ever since he died."

"Why?"

"In his will, Hayden left some money to Conrad and Roberta, but everything else went to Mom. Roberta wanted more money and took mom to court but she lost. Since then they've accused mom of talking Hayden into lowering the amount of money they were to receive and they tell her they know she killed him."

"They accused her of murder?"

"Yes." Carla nodded. "They said that she'd stolen Conrad's inheritance and the settlement that Roberta should have received. When mom ignored them, they started leaving messages and sending letters to Monica and me and telling us mom was a murderer and that all the insurance money and business money she had inherited should go to them instead of us when she died."

"Did they go to the police?" Adam asked.

"Of course not. They had no proof. He died of a heart attack."

"When was the last time you saw or talked with them?"

"My mother talked with my step-brother yesterday and he said that they aren't the ones we should be worrying about."

"What did he mean by that?" Jenna asked.

"Mom and I don't know but it sounded like a threat."

"Could one of them have been at your party?"

"I like to think I would have noticed them but we were having too much fun."

"Plus, they may have hired someone to leave the note." Adam pointed out.

"Do you have an address and phone number for them?" Jenna asked.

"No. Why do you ask?"

"We can go talk to them, see if they know anything."

"I guess I could ask Mom." Carla's phone pinged. She took it out of her purse and looked at it. "Good. It's the list from the caterers. I'll forward it to you both."

Adam's phone vibrated in his pocket. He pulled it out and looked at the name and number. He walked away from the women so they could continue talking.

"Hi, Mason. How was your flight?"

104

"The usual. Drunk passengers, obnoxious businessmen, crying kids. All the reasons I love my job."

Adam laughed. He liked Mason's sense of humour. "When are you coming back?"

"There has been a change of schedules and I'll be home tomorrow. Do you want to get together for lunch?"

"Sure, but you'll have to come to Granville Island. I can't be gone too long from the store."

"No problem. Where do you want to meet?"

"Bridges."

"Okay, I'll be there about 12:30."

Adam hung up and smiled as he walked back to the counter.

"Mason's back," Jenna said.

"Almost. Tomorrow."

"And you're meeting him for lunch."

"Yes."

"I'm glad for you." Jenna grinned impishly. "And maybe you can find out something new for us."

"It's just a friendly lunch." Adam wasn't sure how much he liked this sleuthing gig. It meant you had to be sneaky around your friends in order to gather information. And that wasn't him.

"Are you seeing Mason?" Carla asked, looking up from her phone.

"Not really seeing, but we have met up."

"Just a warning. He's a shit-disturber. He likes to use people's indiscretions against them."

That was one of the first things Adam had learned about Mason. He glanced at Jenna wondering if she had said anything about Bruce's short affair. She shook her head slightly. "Thank you for the heads-up," he said.

"Okay, I've sent the list to both of you," Carla said, putting her cell phone in her purse. She looked at Adam. "Don't get too attached to him. He likes to play the field. Now, I have to go to work. I'll call you later, Jenna."

Adam pulled up the list on his phone. He read over the names and none of them were familiar, not that any should be. He didn't know anyone in the catering business.

The door opened and three women entered. Adam smiled at them as they went past the counter to the mystery section. He turned to Jenna. "Recognize anyone's name?"

"No." Jenna shook her head. "I really didn't expect to. I just wanted Carla to go through it and see if she did."

Adam bit his lip. Something Carla had said bothered him.

"What?" Jenna asked.

"I'm wondering about what Carla said about Mason."

"About him being a shit disturber? I think we know that from him telling you about Bruce and Linda."

"And the other."

"That he doesn't stay in relationships very long?" Jenna asked.

"Yes. It's one thing to hear him say it and another to hear someone else confirm it."

"He might have been saying it just to keep you at arm's length until he got to know you better."

"And if he didn't like me he could use it as a reason to not see me anymore," Adam said, sadly. "I may have to accept that I probably don't have a chance at a relationship with him."

"So, does this mean you have some feelings for him?"

"I hadn't thought so until I talked to him earlier. I was happy to hear his voice. And that's after only one meeting. I guess I need you to explain his reasoning for his lack of commitment so I'm prepared."

"Well, some people get bored easily, like when you watch the same show over and over again. You just get tired of it after a while. Mason seems to be exhibiting behavior known as monkey branching."

"Monkey branching? That's a funny term."

"Yes. In the jungle, a monkey will swing from one tree branch to another without touching the ground. People like Mason fly from one relationship to another without taking the time to touch ground and get to know the person they are dating."

"So, how do you tell if you're dating that type of person?"

"The first one is that the person has a lot of ex-partners."

"Not a good start."

"They like to flirt."

"Well, he did approach me at the party."

"Here are some things to watch for in the future. He won't introduce you to his friends and won't be interested in meeting your friends."

"If we get that far I'll know not to get serious." Adam smiled at his business partner. He was glad to have Jenna on his side.

CHAPTER 13

"So why would Roberta hold a grudge against you for almost twenty years? After all, Hayden was divorced when you met him." Carla had left work, bought some sandwiches, and was now sitting at her mother's table. She had questions about her mother's past that bothered her, questions she hadn't had the nerve to ask before. But, under the present circumstances, she needed some answers. Hers and Bruce's future depended on finding out who had written that note.

"Well, not quite." Becky had her leg propped up on a chair. She reached for a sandwich.

"What do you mean?" Carla distinctly remembered Hayden had said he was divorced when she first met him.

Becky blushed. "Well, it could be because Hayden and I were having an affair while he was still married to her."

Carla stared open-mouthed at her mother. "You what?"

"I basically stole him from her."

This was not something Carla could comprehend. She had always thought her mother hadn't had any boyfriends while she and Monica were growing up, that she was a quiet, mousy, sexless woman whose main goal in life was to provide for her daughters. And now she'd learned that she had slept with a married man and caused his divorce. Becky was a femme fatale, a homewrecker, a seducer.

How many other men had been in her life that Carla didn't know about? Becky had seemed open about her life with her daughters but every once in a while since they'd grown up, she'd say something that shed a fresh light on her as a woman. This was a new disclosure and Carla wondered how many more skeletons were in Becky's closet that she hadn't talked about.

"So, that's why Roberta hates us," Carla said. Officially, it hadn't been her mother who broke up the marriage. It had been Hayden who'd been seeing another woman.

"Well, it's only me she should be hating but she feels you and Monica have taken away Conrad's rightful inheritance."

"Have you tried to explain there is no money?"

"Many times but they don't believe me."

"You haven't told them that you made some provisions for your step-son in your will?" Though there was little money to be divided, Becky had indicated that a third of it should go to Conrad.

Becky swallowed her bite of sandwich. Carla watched as she decided on how to answer.

"I've thought about it hoping it would get them off my back but so far I haven't said anything."

Carla was relieved. She didn't like the idea of Becky telling Conrad. Not because of the money but because of the fact that she didn't really trust Roberta or Conrad. What would they do if they knew about the will? Would they want the money now?

"Who else knows about what's in your will?" When Hayden died, her mother had asked her to be executor of her will. It had been updated when she sold the shoe stores and opened her vintage clothing store.

"Monica asked about it a few months ago."

"She did? Did she say why?"

"No. She just wondered when I'd last updated it."

Carla had no idea why her sister would want to know that. She would have to ask her.

Becky's cell phone chimed showing that someone had buzzed her from downstairs. Carla looked at her mother. "Are you expecting someone?" She hadn't thought of her mom's plans when she'd phoned and said she was coming over with lunch.

"No." Becky said. She pushed a button on her phone. "Hello?"

Carla could hear the person on the other end. "Becky Saunders?"

"Who is this?"

"My name is Abigail Saunders. I'm Hayden's daughter."

"What?" Becky looked in astonishment at Carla.

"Your late husband is my father."

"Keep her talking," Carla mouthed at Becky. She dashed out the door and to the elevator. She pushed the button and waited impatiently. When it didn't come immediately, she jabbed at the button until the doors finally opened. On the ground floor, she took a couple of deep breaths then slowly stepped out when the door opened into the foyer. She saw a young woman standing on the other side of the glass door talking into the intercom.

Carla took in the shoulder length blonde hair, the black skinny jeans, and the matching black jacket over a white blouse. She wore brown, knee-high boots and carried a small, brown purse. Carla casually walked to the door and pushed it open.

"I'd like to come up and talk with you," Abigail was saying. She didn't look in Carla's direction.

"I'm Carla, Becky's daughter."

"Oh." Abigail stepped back.

"What are you doing here?" Carla wondered if she should continue holding the door open or let it close. She wasn't sure if Abigail might try to get by her.

"Conrad told me about my dad's second wife and I wanted to meet her."

"Why?" She decided to hold the door.

"I ..." Abigail seemed close to tears. "I'm sorry." She turned to go then spun back. "Conrad warned me about you, said that you probably wouldn't want to see me," she said boldly. "I guess he was right."

Carla was sympathetic and angry at the same time. Sympathetic for Abigail who obviously believed Conrad's side of the story, and angry that Conrad had set Carla, her mother, and Monica up. "Wait."

"What? You want to yell at me some more?"

"I wasn't yelling. It's just that you startled Mom and me."

"Carla," Becky's voice came through the intercom. "Bring her up."

Carla pushed the door open farther and let Abigail pass. They walked silently to the elevator. Carla pressed the button and they waited for the doors to open. It was a quiet ride to the ninth floor. Carla opened Becky's door and motioned Abigail inside.

Becky held out her hand. "Hello, I'm Becky."

"I'm Abigail." She stepped forward into the dining room and shook Becky's hand. "I'm really sorry to have dropped in like this but it's taken me two weeks to get up the nerve to come here."

"Sit down." Becky waved towards the living room.

Abigail went over to the chair and sat while Carla handed her mother her crutches. They walked over and sat on the couch. Carla had a lot of questions she wanted to ask but decided to leave the conversation up to her mother. After all, Hayden had been her husband.

"So, tell me how you found me and why you think Hayden's your father."

Carla admired her mother's calmness in what had to be a shocking situation.

"I don't just think he is. I *know* he is."

Becky leaned forward. "How do you know?"

"Because my mother told me."

"And who's your mother?"

"Mary Spencer."

"Mary?" Becky sat back in her chair as if pushed. She just stared at Abigail.

"Who's Mary Spencer?" Carla asked.

"She was the long-term manager of one of my dad's stores," Abigail answered.

"When did you find out he was your father?" Becky asked, faintly.

"For most of my life, Mom told me my father died when I was a baby. Then she was diagnosed with terminal cancer last year and decided to tell me. I didn't believe her because when I was a kid I sometimes went to work with her and I had met him. He didn't act like he was my dad and he didn't match the image I'd built up in my mind of my father."

"Then how can you be sure he is?" Carla asked.

"I knew I couldn't just show up here and announce he was my father. Mom also told me about Conrad. I looked him up and told him the story. We each did a DNA test and they confirmed he's my half-brother."

So she was the person he'd warned us against, Carla thought. And no wonder he'd gloated. She'd been born while Hayden was married to her mother.

112

$\mathcal{F}$or the second time that day Carla walked into the bookstore looking weary. Jenna wondered what had happened since she'd left that morning.

"Are you okay?" Jenna asked. She motioned for Carla to come around the counter and sit. Adam was poring over new catalogues they'd just received that announced the latest releases by publishing houses across the country. A few people browsed the shelves.

Carla sighed. "I feel like my life is spinning out of control."

"What's happened?"

"I just had a long conversation with my mother and then we had an unexpected visitor." She stopped and gazed into space.

Jenna glanced at Adam who shrugged as if to say 'I don't know what to do.'

When Carla didn't say any more, Jenna prompted, "Tell me about the conversation."

Carla took a deep breath. "I've told you about mom marrying Hayden when I was in my teens and how he died last year. His ex-wife, Roberta, has always been mad at us over the money he left her and their son, Conrad. I wondered if maybe Roberta and Conrad might be behind this note so I asked Mom why Roberta had been so mad at her for marrying Hayden since they were already divorced. And Mom dropped the bombshell that they hadn't been divorced and that she and Hayden had been having an affair before he left Roberta and married her."

"Oh," Jenna said, not knowing how else to comment.

"My mother is a homewrecker."

Again Jenna looked to Adam for something to say. Again he was quiet. "That was a long time ago," she said.

"Yes," Carla agreed. "But Roberta and Conrad have been harassing us for years because of it." She grimaced. "But they now are having the last laugh."

"How so?" Adam asked.

"Apparently, Hayden wasn't faithful to Mom either. He had an affair with the manager of one of their stores and she had a daughter, Abigail, who he supported for years. Abigail came while I was at Mom's today and wanted to meet her."

This time Jenna had nothing to say to Carla's announcement. They sat in silence, broken when a customer came to the counter to buy three books. Adam stepped to the cash register. The woman had her own bag so Jenna didn't have to help. She and Carla sat quietly but Jenna's mind was racing. Did any of what she'd learned have anything to do with the note or was it just the sign of another family with secrets?

"Are you sure she's his daughter?" Adam asked. "Anyone can claim to be related to someone."

"She said she found Conrad and they did DNA tests. They showed that she and Conrad shared the same father. He told her all about mom and Monica and me and where mom lived. It took her a couple of weeks to get up the nerve to try and talk with mom."

"Did she say why she wanted to meet your mom?" Adam asked. "After all, they aren't related."

"She said she wanted to learn more about her dad and hoped mom could tell her about him."

"How did she come across?" Jenna asked. "Did she seem honest? Did her answers have a ring of truth? Or did they sound rehearsed?"

"Why do you ask? Do you think she could by lying?"

"Did she sound like she was lying to you?"

Carla slowly shook her head. "I was so shocked by what she was saying I never really paid attention to how she was saying it." She cocked her head at Jenna. "What are you thinking?"

"Just wondering if this could be a scheme cooked up by Roberta and Conrad. Could they have hired a woman to play the part of Hayden's illegitimate daughter to get back at your mother for stealing Hayden from them?"

"Why would they do that after all these years?" Carla asked.

"So the woman would be old enough to carry on the deception. A kid or teenager wouldn't be able to do the DNA test or maintain the role in the face of a lot of questions."

"I suppose they could have," Carla said slowly. "Mom says she hasn't had anything to do with them for a long time and I haven't seen or heard from them either. Maybe they've been quiet because of working on this."

"Did she have the DNA test with her?"

"No. I asked and she said she'd forgotten it."

"It seems like a coincidence, her showing up now. Could she have been the woman in the picture?" Jenna asked.

"Oh." Carla pulled out her cell phone and brought up the blurry picture showing a woman bending over the head table. She studied the shot which showed only half of the woman. "I don't think so. Abigail is slimmer than this woman."

"Well, if she was in disguise they could have added some pounds," Adam said.

"Yes." Carla nodded.

"The problem is we don't even know if the woman in the picture was leaving the note," Jenna said.

"But Abigail is a face you can look for in the photos of your engagement party," Adam added.

"Good idea." Carla stood. "I feel better now that I've talked with you two. It's time to go back to my office and get some work done."

Jenna watched her friend leave. Carla hadn't given her a phone number for her step-brother or his mother. Now with this new information she didn't know what to do. She didn't want to go intruding into something that went beyond the note. She'd wait a couple of days and then talk with Carla.

Jenna's phone rang. Drake. "Hello."

"Jenna, can you meet me, like, in an hour?"

"Why? What's happening?" This was a strange request. Usually, they made arrangements a few days in advance.

"I phoned Mrs. Hiscock again and she finally consented to meet with me, but not alone. She wants to bring her sister. I agreed and said I had a friend who would join us, also."

"Where?" Jenna couldn't take much time away from the store.

"The Market Grill there on Granville Island."

"I'll check with Adam." Jenna put her phone on mute.

"What do you want to check with me about?" Adam asked.

"Drake has found a woman who might have some information about Jonathon's death. He wants me to meet them at the Market Grill."

"Yes. Go."

116

"Thank you." Jenna was grateful to Adam. There was no way she wanted to miss this. She unmuted her phone. "Yes. I'll be there."

"I knew you would."

"And how did you know that?"

"You've always been here for me since this whole terrible situation happened. And ..."

Jenna could hear the smile in his voice.

"... you can't resist a good mystery."

An hour later Jenna walked into the Market Grill. She saw Drake with two women and went to their table. Drake stood and held her chair for her. She sat down and he made introductions.

"Mrs. Hiscock and Mrs. Warner, this is my friend Jenna."

Jenna shook hands with the older women who looked like they might be twins. Each had short grey hair with a bright pink streak across the front. Mrs. Hiscock was dressed in black jeans and a purple sweater while her sister had on light blue slacks and a blue blouse.

"I've order dry ribs and potato skins for all of us," Drake said. "Would you ladies like anything to drink?"

"Water, please," Jenna said.

"Coffee for me," the sisters said in unison.

Drake signaled the server and also ordered a coke for himself.

"I was just about to tell them Jonathon's story," Drake said.

Mrs. Hiscock sat with her arms crossed in front of her. "Then get to it. And tell me what it all that has to do with my son Sean and my step-son Gavin."

"It's a long story," Drake started.

"I'm listening."

Jenna ate a potato skin while Drake told the story of his nephew's death as he was crossing the street in a marked crosswalk.

"Oh, I've seen the story on the news," Mrs. Hiscock said. She had uncrossed her arms and was leaning them on the table. "His parents have really done a great job at getting the message out about driving drunk. But what does this have to do with Sean and Gavin?"

"Last spring, your son Sean was taken to the emergency room where I work with overdose patients. I was the one who gave him Naloxone. Gavin came in and was very upset with him. Anyway, a week later my brother and sister-in-law put on a memorial fair for the ten-year anniversary of Jonathon's death. A man wearing a baseball cap and glasses approached Jenna and slipped a note into her hand with his phone number on it. She gave the note to me and I called and left a message. He returned my call and we agreed to meet. He never showed up."

Drake paused and Mrs. Hiscock raised her eyebrows.

"The man who gave Jenna the phone number had a spider tattoo on his neck and I remembered that both your sons had a similar tattoo."

"What are you accusing my sons of?" Mrs. Hiscock demanded.

"Nothing." Drake held up his hands. "I think one of them, probably Gavin because of his age, might have some information about my nephew's death."

"Because someone with a spider tattoo gave Jenna a phone number?"

"Yes."

"That doesn't prove anything. There are hundreds, if not thousands, of such tattoos in the city."

Jenna could see the defeat start to hit Drake. Obviously this woman was not going to be much help.

"Do you remember Gavin ever mentioning the name Trevor?" Drake asked.

"No. Why?"

"Before the man gave Jenna the note, someone came up to me and said that the driver of the car had been the younger brother of his friend. The brother's name was Trevor and he lived in Richmond. The man suddenly left without telling me more."

"Trevor might be someone Gavin knew from ten years ago," Jenna prompted.

"I don't know Gavin's friends now, let alone the ones he had ten years ago. Besides, he hasn't lived with us for years."

"Do you have a phone number I can call to try and talk with him?" Drake asked.

"I do, but it won't do you any good to call it. It's not in service anymore. Gavin probably got a new number and didn't let us know."

"May I have it anyway?"

Mrs. Hiscock pulled out her cell phone and opened it. She scrolled through and found his name and number. She showed it to Drake. He put it in his phone. Jenna couldn't tell if he recognized it or not.

"What about Sean?" Drake asked. "He would have been quite young ten years ago but do you think Gavin might have said something to him? They seemed pretty close."

The woman hesitated. "I haven't seen Sean since last spring. When my husband found out he had tried drugs and almost died from an overdose, the two had a big fight. Sean moved out. I've left messages on his cell but so far he hasn't gotten back to me.

I've been waiting ever since the fight for either Sean or my husband to cool down and contact the other but both are too stubborn."

"You said in our last conversation that you didn't think the man found by the police was either of your sons. Did you tell the police that?"

"Yes. They want me to do a DNA test. I haven't gone down to the station yet."

"So, you still believe that."

"I'm sure it's neither of them."

"But you haven't seen or heard from them in months."

"Both of them are fine," Mrs. Hiscock said emphatically. "Gavin is busy and Sean is mad at us. They'll come around to see us soon."

Jenna felt sorry for the woman. It was obvious she was in denial. She had her fears but didn't want to admit it might be one of her sons. "We'll go to the police with you," she offered.

Mrs. Hiscock stood abruptly. "It's neither of them. It's one of the hundreds of people who have the same tattoo." She hurried away.

"I've been trying to get her to go but she's scared," Mrs. Warner said. She followed her sister.

Drake propped his elbows on the table and dropped his head in his hands. "What should we do now?" he asked dismally.

"I guess the only thing we can do is wait." Jenna hated to hear the dejection in Drake's voice. "Like Mrs. Hiscock said, there are plenty of people who have that tattoo and the police never mentioned where on the body it was located."

"You're right." Drake raised his head. "I feel like this was a total waste of time. We don't know any more than we did an hour ago." He took his wallet out of his pocket, set some money on the table, and stood.

"What about the phone number, Mrs. Hiscock? Do you recognize it?"

"I think I might still have the paper you were given with the phone number on it. I'll look for it when I get home and see if it's the same. I'll let you know."

"Okay."

"Thank you for coming tonight on such short notice," Drake said, as they walked out of the restaurant. "I wanted you here as moral support."

Jenna was glad that he still considered her his friend and confidant. "You're welcome," she said, climbing into her car.

CHAPTER 14

"**W**hat do you think about us having a step-sister?" Monica demanded, walking into Carla's office.

"Mom told you?" Carla put down her pen and sat back.

"Boy, did she ever. What a phone call we had." Monica dropped into the chair in front of Carla's desk. "Plus, she told me about her stealing Hayden away from Roberta."

"Quite the story."

"Yes, it almost made me feel sorry for Roberta and Conrad. It's hard to blame them for the harassment over the years."

"'Almost' being the operative word," Carla said. "That was their choice to make."

"How old is this Abigail?"

"She looks to be about the same age I was when we met Hayden."

"So, either he was seeing Mary Spencer and Mom at the same time, or he took up with her soon after he and mom married. Oh, poor Mom. That must have been a shock to have her turn up out of the blue like that."

"She actually handled it a lot better than I would have. She was quite civil to her."

"So what's she like?"

"She has blonde hair—not sure if it's real or not. She was mainly quiet, which could have been because of just meeting us but she did answer our questions."

"Does she look like Hayden or Conrad at all?"

"I didn't notice any real resemblance but she could take after her mother. I asked Mom that after Abigail left and Mom said Mary had natural blonde hair and was about the same height. It seemed Mom looked after the store she managed while Hayden handled the other two. She only met the other managers and employees at their annual Christmas parties, summer barbeques, and the occasional team meetings."

"Who did she get the DNA test through? Mom said she didn't have the test results with her."

"I think it was Ancestry DNA. And she said she will bring it the next time she and mom meet."

"There's going to be a next time?" Monica asked.

"Abigail wants one but mom didn't commit to it."

"So, what are we going to do?"

"I don't think there is much we can do. It's in mom's hands now."

"I sure hope Abigail doesn't feel she's entitled to Mom's money like Roberta and Conrad do." Monica said, resentfully. "I don't think mom owes any of them anything."

"I don't either, but it's her money." Carla paused. She wasn't sure if she should mention it but she did need to know. "Which does bring up the topic of mom's will. She said you asked her about it a while ago."

"Yes." Monica blushed a little.

"Why?"

"She's getting older and we'll have to look after her soon. I know you're her executor but I just wanted to know what we're dealing with."

"And?"

"What 'and'?"

"What else did you want? Are you having money troubles?"

Carla felt a huge disappointment when she saw Monica's shoulder's slump. It had been a guess but she'd been right. "Did you ask Mom for money?"

"No," Monica said, indignantly.

"Were you going to?"

"I was going to ask for some of my inheritance."

"But you found out there isn't as much money as you thought."

"What happened to their money? After all, they owned three stores."

"Apparently, Hayden liked to spend money, so they didn't have much of a nest egg. It took most of their savings to give Roberta and Conrad the money Hayden left them in his will and to pay for his funeral. And they only owned the merchandise and rented the store space. When mom sold, she barely received the value of the shoes and equipment and some business goodwill."

"So, how was she able to open her vintage clothing store?"

"I'm a silent partner."

"Oh. She never told me any of this."

"I think she's embarrassed at how little she and Hayden had after all the years of working. The only reason she told me this was because I'm her executor." Carla paused a moment then asked gently. "What do you need money for? Maybe I can help."

"I want to start my own business."

"Doing what?" Carla didn't know what type of business a dental assistant could open.

"I want to start my own production company and write and put on plays. I've already written three stage plays that I think are really good."

"Oh." Carla was surprised. She knew Monica liked the theatre, she just hadn't known how much.

Monica leaned forward in her chair. "I've spent weekends and evenings learning every aspect about putting on a play. I've sat in on the interviews of potential actors for the performances and watched what it takes to design and make a decent set. I've even talked with the theatre's accountant to learn how money is generated and how it is spent. There's a lot more for me to learn but I can do it."

"Why didn't you come to me instead of Mom?"

"I thought about it, I really did. But I was embarrassed that you've done so much better with your life than I have with mine and I wanted to prove myself. I did chicken out about asking mom. I decided I would try to do it by raising money on my own."

"You know you and Mom are my beneficiaries if something happens to me, so you might as well make use of the money when you need it. I'll put money into your company. I've always loved going to the plays you're in and I think you're an excellent actress."

Monica smiled for the first time. "Really? You think that?"

"Yes and I'm angry that you wouldn't come to me. You're very talented and I am proud of you."

"Thank you," Monica hurried around the desk and hugged her sister. "You won't regret it."

Carla hugged her back. "I know I won't."

"And now I have to get to the theatre and prepare for tonight's performance."

Carla's cell phone rang as she watched her sister leave the office. She picked it up and saw her mother's name.

"Hi, Mom."

"Carla. I just got off the phone with Abigail and she wants us all to meet. You, Monica, and me and her, Conrad, and Roberta."

125

"Well, that was fast. She's not wasting any time. Did she say when?"

"This week."

"I don't think that's a good idea. You can't go out with your leg and I don't want them in your apartment."

"Well, I did say we could meet on Friday for lunch."

"Mom!"

"What? I don't want to draw this out any longer than necessary. Let's get together, agree that she is Hayden's daughter, and have our hour-long talk about him. She'll be satisfied and leave us alone."

"Okay. I'll rent a wheelchair that will support your leg for Friday and come get you."

"I knew you'd help. I'll phone Monica and let her know."

CHAPTER 15

*J*enna rang the buzzer for Carla's condo. She'd phoned and asked if she and Adam could meet with Carla and Bruce. They wanted to ask them both some additional questions and see if they'd learned anything more. Carla buzzed them up and opened the door when they knocked. She was dressed in leggings and an oversized men's shirt. She led them into the living room where Bruce stood by the couch. He wore a pair of blue jeans and a grey, crewneck sweater and appeared more relaxed than when Jenna had last seen him Sunday morning.

"Bruce," Jenna said. After Adam had told her that Bruce had spent time with his ex-girlfriend just a couple of weeks ago, she didn't feel the same warmth towards him she'd felt since Carla so happily introduced them.

"Jenna, Adam," Bruce smiled. "May I take your coats?"

Jenna and Adam shrugged out of their coats and handed them to Bruce. He draped them over the back of a kitchen chair.

"Sit down," Carla said. "As you can see, Bruce and I started without you." She indicated the two half-empty wine glasses on the coffee table. "Would either of you like a glass of wine or a beer?"

"Not for me." Jenna sat on one of the overstuffed chairs. "I'm driving."

"I'll have a beer," Adam said. He took the other chair.

A plate of crackers and cheese sat in the middle of the coffee table and four small plates and a stack of napkins were beside it. Carla came with a can of beer which she placed on a coaster in front of Adam. She handed Jenna a bottle of water. "In case you get thirsty," she smiled. "And help yourselves to some snacks."

Carla and Bruce returned to their places on the couch and Bruce refilled their glasses from the bottle of wine he'd brought from the kitchen. The way they sat side by side made Jenna think they were still a couple. There was a moment of awkward silence then Jenna got to the point of their visit.

"Have you gone through the photos and checked each person in them?" Jenna asked.

"Yes," Carla nodded. "So far we haven't seen anyone we don't know."

"Good. Now, to review: Adam and I are supposed to find out who left that note on the head table but so far none of the photos we've seen shows anything unusual and none of the names on the caterer's list mean anything to either of you so we have to delve further. Sunday, I asked both of you if there was anyone you invited who might have a grudge against you. Both of you said no but since then, Carla has told me about her step-brother and his mother and the aggravation they've caused her mother and subsequently her and her sister. Did you know about them, Bruce?"

"Yes, we don't have secrets from each other. She also told me about her new step-sister."

"Can you tell us if there is anyone you know who might dislike you enough to do this?" Adam asked Bruce. "Someone who wants revenge for something in the past?"

Jenna liked the way Adam worded that. They'd discussed if they should steer the conversation to Ronnie and his date at the engagement party and decided to wait and see what Bruce told them. Jenna certainly didn't want to hurt Carla but she didn't like the fact that Bruce had been unfaithful so soon after asking Carla to marry him. And that made her detest the man himself. She hoped her true feelings wouldn't show while they talked.

"No, I've done a lot of thinking and have come up with no one who would hate me that much."

"Can you tell us a little about yourself, Bruce?"

"I'm an only child. My father died six years ago and my mother is in the early stages of dementia. As Ronnie said at our engagement party, he, Bill, and I have been friends since we were small. I graduated high school and paid my way through college by working at a fast food restaurant. I took a business course and worked my way up to manager of the restaurant. But I wanted to get in on the craft beer industry and eventually I bought one franchise, then a second, and third. And now I'm working on my fourth with Ronnie."

Jenna remembered that his work and business profile on the dating site had been so similar to Carla's that it seemed they would have a lot in common. She reached for a plate and put some crackers and cheese on it.

"I'm not perfect and I know I've made some people mad at me over the years but I don't think any of them would retaliate like this," Bruce finished.

"Have you ever been married?" Adam asked.

"No."

"Any ex-girlfriends who might object to you getting married?" Jenna asked. She was watching for Bruce's reaction but it was Carla who dropped the plate she was holding.

Jenna looked in dismay at Adam while Carla and Bruce picked up the plate and food that had fallen to the floor. She saw the consternation on his face that she felt. Carla knew about Bruce's short affair with Ronnie's cousin and Jenna had just thrown it in her face.

"I'm so sorry," Carla said. "I don't know what happened."

"It's okay, darling," Bruce said. "No harm done. A quick vacuum will get the cracker crumbs." He turned back to Adam and Jenna. "To answer your question, I've never married but have had two long-term relationships, one in my twenties and one up until a year ago. We parted on good terms after five years. And then I met Carla and knew she was the one I've been waiting for." He smiled at Carla.

"Did you and any of your groomsmen ever have a falling out, Bruce?" Adam asked.

Jenna was glad that he had steered the conversation away from ex-girlfriends and onto a different topic.

"Nothing that affected our friendship for very long."

"Can you elaborate?"

"When I was seventeen, I saved all summer to buy a motorcycle. One night when we'd been drinking, I passed out and Ronnie stole my keys and took it for a joy ride. He went around a corner too fast and laid it down. He suffered some road rash on his leg but my motorcycle was all scraped and scratched. I was so mad that I hit him and told him to stay away from me. I felt really bad and I missed him, so within a month I apologized to him and he apologized back and we were friends again. He even gave me some money to fix and repaint it."

Bruce smiled ruefully. "I sold it the next year and bought a car."

"Did he 'borrow' that, too?" Jenna said, making quotation marks around the word borrow.

"Yes, but only with permission."

"What did he borrow it for?"

"He liked to take his dates up to Cypress Mountain Provincial Park and look down on Vancouver and the Lion's Gate Bridge."

Jenna could understand why. It was a spectacular view. "Did he do that often?" It took a good friend to lend someone his car.

"Only when it was a girl he loved."

"Were there many of them?"

"Only one that I knew of."

There was silence for a while, then Adam asked, "Any more Facebook posts?"

"Carla and I keep checking our pages but so far there haven't been any more. Poor Bill. He didn't have access to the old email he set up his Facebook account with and he didn't remember his password so he had to set up a new account and send out new friend requests to everyone. He is sure ticked off with whoever hacked him."

"So, he still has no idea who posted that to his site?"

"No."

"Is there anything else either of you can think of that would make a person leave the threat?" Jenna asked. "It doesn't have to be something big. Sometimes an insult or snub will work on a person's mind until it becomes a big deal to them and they think someone has to pay."

Carla and Bruce looked at each other.

"No," Carla said, shaking her head. "I can't."

"Nothing for me, either," Bruce said.

"Bruce, I am going to ask some personal questions. Who would inherit your estate right now if something happened to you?"

"I've left provisions for my mother and the rest goes to Mason."

"Not his sister, too?"

Bruce was quiet for a few minutes. "Destiny disappeared when she was seventeen."

"Oh." Jenna looked at Adam. Was this the reason Mason hadn't wanted to talk with Adam about her? "I'm sorry Bruce. That must have been hard on your family."

"It was. It still is. We've never learned what happened to her, whether she left on her own or was abducted and murdered."

"The police never discovered anything?"

"No. She had a date that night but no one knew who with. And her body hasn't been found in all these years. But that has nothing to do with what's happening now."

Jenna decided to get back to the original conversation. "Does Mason know he inherits?"

"Yes, and he's agreed to have power of attorney over the money I'm leaving for Mom's care."

"That means Mason gets everything in your will?"

"Yes."

"Were you going to change it once you married Carla?"

"Of course."

"I don't trust him," Carla said, quietly.

"Oh, not this," Bruce moaned. He stood and walked away.

"Why don't you trust him?" Jenna asked, ignoring Bruce's grumble.

"He hates being a flight attendant. He's only working until he can retire with his pension or until he finds a better job. He talks on and on about how he detests the passengers' attitude and their constant complaining about the size of the seats, the length of the flight, and anything else they can think of."

"That doesn't mean he wants to kill me," Bruce said.

132

"We don't know that. What if he doesn't want to lose his inheritance? We know that someone who doesn't want you to marry me left that note."

"Which brings up Conrad and Roberta," Jenna said. "Did you get a phone number for me to contact them?"

"Yes." Carla opened her phone and showed Jenna. "I asked Mom and she thinks they could be behind it just to hassle us. She said it was okay for you to contact them."

"What do you and Monica and your mom think of Abigail?"

"Well, we're all going for lunch on Friday. We thought getting together on neutral ground would be a good thing."

"Are Conrad and Roberta going to be there?"

"Unfortunately, yes. I think Abigail asked them as a kind of buffer for her. I don't think she knows about the misery they've caused us over the years."

Jenna could think of nothing more. She and Adam stood. "We'll continue talking with the others who were at the head table and see what we can learn."

CHAPTER 16

*B*efore going to the bookstore Thursday morning, Adam opened his computer and looked up the name Destiny Devers. There were a number of sites about the seventeen-year-old girl who'd disappeared twenty-five years ago. He clicked on one and read part of the news article:

The Vancouver Police Service are searching for Destiny Devers who was last seen at the Park Royal Shopping Centre where she had gone with friends. When her friends decided to go to a movie, Destiny wanted to stay at the centre and find a pair of shoes before meeting up with her date for the evening. She's described as 5'6", slim build with light brown hair. She was last seen wearing blue jeans, a pink jacket, and white shoes.

There were other sites where the police appealed to the public for any information. There was even an age enhanced drawing from a few years ago that showed what she would look like as an adult in her thirties.

Adam continued to scroll through other sites and was amazed at the long list of missing people in each province. It seemed there were more added each year. He glanced at the clock and quickly shut down his computer. He was going to be late. He dashed out of his condo and down to the bus stop. He didn't own a car, feeling that the expense of buying, insuring, maintenance, and fuel wasn't worth it. He rode the bus wherever he had to go and if in a hurry, called a cab.

When he arrived at the store, Jenna had already opened it and there were two customers browsing the shelves.

"Sorry," he said. "I got caught up looking at websites about Destiny Devers." Adam brought one up on his cell phone and showed it to Jenna. "I found this."

Jenna read it over then handed back his phone. "It must be difficult for the family since the police have never been able to solve what happened to her. They don't even know if she's alive or dead."

"Yes, but there's still hope. I read one site about a car being found in Griffin Lake near Revelstoke, B.C. The woman inside had been missing for twenty-five years. Every year or two the police put out a request for anyone having information about Destiny to come forward. Maybe eventually someone will."

The morning was busy and at twelve o'clock, Adam left to walk down Duranleau St. to Bridges to meet Mason. Even though he knew he had to take it slow because of Carla's and Jenna's warnings, he was excited about seeing Mason again.

Mason was at the table when Adam arrived. This time, he stood and came around to greet him. He had on a white t-shirt with 'Into the Wine, Not the Label' on the front. Adam recognized it as being from the television show, *Schitt's Creek*, and it acknowledged the character, David's, pansexuality. He gave Adam a quick hug. "It's good to see you again."

Adam was touched at Mason's affectionate greeting. "I'm glad you came back early."

They sat down and Adam saw that Mason had already ordered them both Moscow Mule Mimosas.

"I know you have to go back to the bookstore but I thought we should have a celebratory drink."

"What are we celebrating?" Adam was hesitant about having a drink at lunch. He didn't want to go back to the store smelling of liquor. That really wouldn't impress the customers.

"Our second date." Mason picked up his glass and held it up.

"Our second date." Adam wasn't sure if he would call these two get-togethers true dates but he raised his glass and they clinked. He took a sip and set his down.

"I've already ordered our lunch," Mason said.

"Oh?" Adam cocked his head. He had a favourite dish he liked here and usually ordered it.

"Don't worry," Mason grinned. "I called Jenna and asked her what you liked and she told me about the tuna tacos. I requested those for both of us, so they would be ready when you arrived."

"Thank you." Adam was a little surprised at Mason's thoughtfulness. He himself hadn't thought about phoning ahead to place his order. But then again, he knew he could be a little late getting back. Jenna had told him to take his time and enjoy the lunch.

"I hear you and Jenna are still trying to find out about the note," Mason said.

"Yes, there isn't much to go on. The photos people took don't show anything unusual and it doesn't look like someone from the catering did it. We're going to talk to the rest of the head table."

"I hope that's not why you agreed to see me again today," Mason pouted.

"No," Adam said, hastily. "I really wanted to see you on my own."

"Good, because I told you all I knew last time. And I didn't take any pictures."

Adam took another sip of his drink. He had no idea what to talk about. According to Carla, Mason hated his job, so that was out.

"Tell me how you came to own a bookstore," Mason said, leaning forward and resting his forearms on the table.

That was a subject Adam felt comfortable talking about and he smiled as he told Mason about meeting Jenna in university and their shared interest in books. He told him about the jobs they'd had until they saved enough money to buy the store.

"Sounds as if you're living your dream," Mason said.

"Pretty much. What about you? Is being a flight attendant living your dream?" He was impressed with the way he had segued into learning more about what Carla had told them.

"Not really," Mason grimaced. "When I first started, I enjoyed flying around the world, seeing new places and learning history, but now it's gotten boring."

"I can't imagine travelling is boring."

"It is when you really can't have a life at home."

Adam thought back to their first conversation about Mason's job. He'd blamed it for not sticking to a relationship for very long.

"Have you thought about trying something different?"

"At my age?" Mason snorted. "Companies don't want to start training someone in their forties. They want younger people who will be with them for years."

Adam wondered if this was the place to get more information. Because even though Mason had told him he had nothing more to contribute, Jenna and Adam had found out differently.

"What?" Mason asked.

Might was well jump right in. "Bruce said you inherit if he dies."

Mason sat back in his chair. "Really? You're asking me if I would kill him so I could inherit his money?"

"No." Adam quickly held up his hands. "I'm just confirming what he said. You'll also have power of attorney over the money he sets aside for his mother's care."

"Yes. And all that changes when he marries Carla. In fact, we've already been to the lawyer to get the papers drawn up for me to relinquish my power of attorney."

The server came with their meals. He set the plates in front of each of them. "May I get you anything else?"

"No, we're fine," Mason smiled up at him.

Adam was happy to see that Mason had calmed down. He decided to try a different approach in his questioning. "What can you tell me about Ronnie?" He picked up one of the tacos and took a bite. It tasted delicious as always.

"I've known Ronnie since I used to visit Bruce. We never really developed a friendship and I haven't seen much of him over the years." Mason took a drink from his glass then a bite of one of his tacos. "Oh, I can tell why these are your favourite here," he mumbled, around his food.

"What about Bill?"

"I've only seen him a few times since we grew up. I never really cared for the guy. He was always a little pushy."

"Pushy? In what way?" Adam had another sip of his drink. He did like the taste.

"He was always trying to set me up with his sister when we were younger."

"Did he know you were gay?"

"No. I wasn't even admitting to myself that I was, and I actually dated a few girls."

"Did you go out with his sister?"

"Once. We went to a movie and then for a burger. She was very perceptive and when I walked her home she told me that she was not the type of romantic interest I really wanted. Up until then, I'd thought I was hiding it well but I realized that many family and friends already knew or at least suspected so I decided to come out. It was kind of anticlimactic since it didn't surprise many."

"What do you think of Bill now?"

"He hasn't changed. Two weeks ago, he asked all of the head table and families over to his place for a barbeque. His sister was there and he reintroduced us and told me that she had been divorced twice but was unattached now. Talk about embarrassing for both of us."

Adam nodded, not sure what to say. "Bruce told me about your sister, Destiny and how she never came home after a date."

Mason paused in taking a bite of his taco. "And?"

"I know it was a long time ago but I just want to offer my sympathy. That couldn't have been easy on your family."

"It wasn't. It still isn't. It probably never will be." Mason signaled the server. "Did you make the Mule?" he asked.

"Yes, I sometimes step behind the bar," he said. "Is something wrong with it?"

"Oh, no," Mason smiled. "It's the best I've tasted. You have a talent."

"Thank you." The server gave a slight bow.

"May I ask your name?"

"It's Wayne."

"Well, Wayne, I'm Mason and I'd like another Mule."

Wayne looked at Adam.

"No, one is enough." Adam felt a slight discomfort. Had Mason just flirted with the server? Maybe he should get away from the questioning for a while and treat this like the date it was supposed to be.

"Do you like to travel outside of work?"

"No, actually. You might say I'm a homebody. I like to walk the English Bay Seawall, suntan at the beach, go for coffee with friends."

Wayne returned with Mason's drink. He kept eye contact with Mason and smiled as he set it down.

Well, so much for a date, Adam thought. Even though Mason had partially turned his head, Adam had seen the wink.

"Tell me about your coming out," Mason said, turning back to Adam. "Was it traumatic?"

Adam smiled ruefully. It wasn't something he usually talked about. "My parents, especially my dad, weren't happy when I finally came out as being gay at thirteen. My mother eventually accepted it but my father became distant almost to the point of not treating me like a son anymore. Luckily, my siblings didn't care. However, one aunt and uncle and my cousins made my life miserable for years, suggesting that I go for conversion therapy or attend church and repent.

"They kept bringing me pamphlets to read and recommending websites for my parents and me to check out. My parents didn't agree to do any of that and my mother finally told them to stop. I couldn't wait to get away from there and I applied to the UBC here in Vancouver. Before I left home to move here, my father hugged me and told me he loved me no matter what. That was the first time he'd said anything about my orientation."

"Sounds tough."

"It was, but I'm over it now."

"How many times have you gone back to visit and how many times have your parents been here to see you?"

Adam felt himself blush. "Twice for me and once for my parents."

"Did you visit your aunt and uncle?" Mason asked with a grin.

"No." Adam said tersely.

"What?"

"They moved to Connaught Heights in New Westminster seven years ago. And, yes, they've asked and, no, I haven't seen them since they came."

"What about your siblings?"

"My brother lives in Whitehorse, Yukon, and my sister in Kamloops here in British Columbia."

"Do you see much of them?"

"No." Adam wasn't interested in continuing this conversation. Time to get back on topic. "Do you think Bruce might have placed that note to get out of marrying Carla?"

"Are you crazy?" Mason looked shocked. "Why would you ask that?"

"It's a possibility."

"No, it's not. Bruce loves Carla. He wants to marry her."

"What about his fling with Linda? That doesn't sound like a man in love and wanting to get married."

"You're not going to leave it alone, are you?"

Adam shrugged. "Just trying to help a friend get a feel for who might have written the note. So Bruce still wants to go through with the wedding?"

"Yes."

"Even knowing two former fiancés have died?"

Mason sighed. "One was killed in a robbery, which happens often enough in Vancouver, and one fell off his balcony, which happens occasionally when someone is drunk."

"Have they set a date?"

"No. Apparently, Carla wants to find out who sent the note before she goes much further. She's the one who's really worried."

"Yes." Adam knew how troubled Carla was. She was constantly contacting Jenna with information she'd learned, or something she'd thought of, or sending more photos. He glanced at his watch. Time to go. He reached for his wallet in his pocket.

Mason held up his hand. "It's on me." He signaled Wayne.

"That's not necessary." Adam stood as Wayne came over with the card machine.

"I invited you." Mason also stood. "Besides, it's entertaining to watch a sleuth at work."

"Not really a sleuth," Adam said, thinking that he hadn't learned much.

Mason pushed the buttons to add a tip to the bill and then tapped the machine with his card. After a few seconds, it came up not approved.

"What?" Mason exclaimed. He then inserted the card and went through the same process typing in his pin number. Again, not approved showed up on the screen.

"What the hell? Something must be wrong with your machine." Mason took some bills from his wallet and handed the money to Wayne. "Keep the change," he said, with a smile.

Adam knew the prices of the tacos and the drinks and saw that Mason had just left a hefty tip.

"Do you want a ride back to the store?" Mason asked.

"No, thank you. I have to stop and pick up some fruit at the market."

They headed towards the door.

"Enjoy your day," Wayne said.

"You, too." Adam turned slightly to answer. He saw Mason and Wayne's hands touch. Had Wayne just handed Mason a piece of paper?

"Thank you for the lunch," Adam said, when they reached Mason's car.

"We have to do this again, maybe make an evening of it. But, no questions next time."

"Sounds good. Bye."

As Adam walked in the direction of the market, he thought about how amazed he was when he heard about some peoples' lives and the family and friends who shared them. Carla's philanderer of a step-father, her step-brother, and now a step-sister, and her fiancés and their untimely deaths. The relationship between Bruce, his cousin, and his two friends, his affair with Linda, and the disappearance of Mason's sister. Both Carla and Bruce were successful but both seemed to be lonely. And now, Mason with his talk about his coming out. Once Adam had moved and begun his new life, he hadn't thought much about who he would fall in love with and who he wouldn't.

At the market, Adam bought some strawberries and bananas. They were a quick snack when they got busy.

"So, tell me how it went," Jenna said, when Adam was settled behind the counter. "Was it good?"

"He had a drink and my favourite meal ordered when I got there, thanks to you."

"He was worried that you didn't have much time so he wanted to make sure you had a chance to eat without being rushed."

"And it worked. The meal came shortly after I arrived."

"You don't sound very happy. Did something go wrong?"

"Well, after he got over being mad at me twice for asking more questions about the note, it went well."

"What did you learn?"

"Mason, Bruce, and Carla went to a lawyer to get the paperwork started to change power of attorney and the beneficiary on Bruce's will so it looks as if there was going to be a change over."

"So he could be worried about losing the inheritance to Carla."

"Right and his credit card was declined twice. I looked up what a flight attendant earns and it ranges from twenty-one to fifty-five dollars an hour."

"Not that much to survive on in Vancouver. He could be getting desperate and is using Carla's past to get rid of Bruce. Anything else?"

"He dated girls before he admitted he was gay. He doesn't like Bill because Bill used to try and set him up with his sister when they were young and even recently at a barbeque."

"Even though he knows Mason is gay?"

"Apparently."

"So, Carla doesn't like Mason and Mason doesn't like Bill. Doesn't sound like a happy bunch of people."

"And I doubt I'll be seeing him again."

"Oh? Why?"

"He flirted with the server, Wayne, in front of me, left him a hefty tip, and I saw Wayne give him a piece of paper as we were leaving."

"Not good."

"No, but Carla did warn me and you explained what to watch for so I'm not all that disappointed." Adam changed subjects. "There's something I've been wondering. What if Carla decided she didn't want to marry Bruce after all or maybe it was Bruce who got cold feet? Leaving a note like that would give both of them an excuse to call off the wedding."

"But why at their own party?" Jenna asked. "Why not before they had a big party to announce their engagement?"

"No guts. One of them got too far into this relationship too quickly and couldn't figure out how to back out gracefully."

"I guess we'll have to ask each of them."

"Yes, but now you have to go for lunch."

"Right. I called Hillary at her salon to let her know her books came in. We're meeting at the café."

CHAPTER 17

Jenna walked to the café in the centre atrium of the Loft. There was always a steady stream of visitors to the businesses in the building and many stopped for a light meal at the café. Usually, it was impossible to find a table during the lunch hour but she saw that Hillary had already snagged one.

She hurried over and set the bag on the table. "I'll go get us each a sandwich. What kind do you want?"

"Egg salad on whole wheat, if they have one, and a bottle of water."

Jenna got in line at the counter and soon returned with two sandwiches and two bottles of water.

"What kind did you get?" Hillary asked, as Jenna set hers on the table then sat down.

"Pastrami on rye." Jenna opened the package.

"Oh, I can smell it," Hillary laughed.

"Well, yours isn't a bouquet of flowers either."

"So how is the descrambling going?" Hillary took a bite from her sandwich. "Have you been able to figure out who left the note?"

"No. The photos we've seen so far don't show anyone near the table. We're checking to see if any of the bridesmaids or groomsmen had a reason to threaten Bruce. We're sure digging up a lot of information about Carla's and Bruce's past."

"Oh? What?"

"There are some people from Carla's side who may have it in for her. Bruce spent a few nights with his former girlfriend after he and Carla got engaged."

"What? You're kidding me."

"I wish I was. And get this—she's the cousin of Bruce's best friend and best man, Ronnie, and Ronnie took her to the engagement party as his date."

"Oh, how awful for Carla. Does she know?"

"I don't know. Adam and I had a talk with Bruce and Carla and we did ask him if there were any girlfriends who might object to his marrying Carla. He said no but Carla dropped her plate of food."

"So, she might know about it."

"That's what we thought. I'm going to have to ask Bruce about it when I talk to him alone."

"When's that?"

"So far we've settled on a late lunch here on Saturday."

"Drake told me about the spider tattoo and your meeting with a Mrs. Hiscock."

"Yes," Jenna grimaced. "He's really trying hard to make a connection between the boys he saw in the hospital with the tattoos and Jonathon's killer."

"Do you think there is one?"

"I hope for his sake that there is. Tell me what's new since I saw you at the engagement party."

"Not much. The salon is doing well and Drake and I are enjoying each other's company."

"That's all? Just enjoying each other's company?"

"We're taking it slow. What about you? Anyone new in your life I should know about?"

"No, although a new client who came to see me is a hunk. I'd date him if given a chance."

"Tell me about him."

"His name is Ray. He's about my age, blond, really cute and has his own moving business."

"So why does he need a dating coach? Sounds like the type women throw themselves at."

"Well, it's his business that's the problem. It's called 'We Deal In What's Left Behind'."

"Unusual name. What type of business is it?"

"When someone dies and leaves a houseful of furniture and general stuff, he goes in and cleans it all out."

"Ugh, morbid." Hillary shivered then took a drink of her water.

"That's what I thought, too, but he pointed out it's a necessary occupation. Not everyone has the time or the ability to be dispassionate enough to clean out a relative's home after they die. To some it is too heartbreaking so they hire him to go in and sort everything into throw away, give away, and sell piles."

"That I can understand," Hillary nodded. "It was hard to go through my aunt's things when she died. So what did you advise him?"

"I said he should only mention that he owned a moving business on the dating site and wait until the third date before telling what it was he actually did."

"So, are you going to let him know you are interested?"

"You know my history with men I've met on those sites. I'm getting tired of trying."

"And that is what makes you such a good coach. You've been on just about every dating site out there."

"Those who can't, teach," Jenna laughed.

"But you've already met him and have gotten to know him a little. He shouldn't disappoint you."

"That's true."

"And look how it will help your business if you show that he found a date so fast. You will prove that you earned your title as a celebrated dating coach."

"'Celebrated' is a lofty word for what I do."

"Well, you certainly have assisted many people find the right person through your coaching."

"That's true," Jenna admitted. "The reason Ray came to me was because I helped his sister find a man who became her husband last year. It was her wedding I went to just after Easter. I actually met Ray there but I didn't recognize him when he came to my office because he had shaved off his mustache."

"So are you going to contact him?"

"I'll be seeing him again this weekend to go through a date scenario."

*J*enna stood in front of the Alliance Theatre and tapped out a text to Monica that she'd arrived. They'd agreed to meet at the theatre because there wasn't a performance that night. Over the years of her and Carla's friendship, Jenna had met Monica at parties and other gatherings. She'd found her serious with a passion for the theatre. She seldom talked about her day job as a dental assistant. The door opened and Monica ushered Jenna inside. She was wearing an old pair of jeans and a shirt that had paint on it.

Jenna stepped into the foyer, which seemed a lot larger than it had when it was crowded the night of the play.

Monica led Jenna into the house. "We're making some changes to the set so we can talk here."

The house had a hushed reverence to it like it was in sleep mode waiting to be awakened by the next performance. Jenna felt like she should tread softly and speak quietly. The spell was broken by the pounding of a hammer. Jenna looked at the stage and saw a number of people doing various tasks.

"Any news on who might have left the paper on the head table?" Monica asked.

"No," Jenna said, as she followed Monica down the aisle and up the four stairs onto the stage.

"Hey everyone," Monica said, loudly. "This is Jenna. We've something to discuss so she'll be here for a while."

The two men and one woman all turned and lifted their hands in a wave.

"Hi, Jenna," the woman said then they went back to their work.

Jenna saw they were trying to align a door in its frame. She looked at the rest of the set and, up close, she could see the little flaws in the construction and painting that weren't noticeable from the seats.

Monica picked up a can of paint and a brush and began painting over what looked like a repaired hole in one of the walls.

"I've come to see if you can think of anyone who would want to scare Bruce away from marrying Carla," Jenna said.

"I've tried and I can't come up with anyone other than Roberta and Conrad, who Carla already told you about."

"And now there's Abigail to add."

"Yes, our step-sister." She indicated a chair on the set. "Make yourself comfortable."

"What do you think of her story?" Jenna asked, sitting down. "Do you think it's a scam?"

"Now that we know Hayden took up with mom while still married to Roberta, it sounds plausible that he wouldn't have been faithful to mom either."

Jenna didn't know enough about the situation to ask any more questions. She went in a different direction. "That's a beautiful ring you helped Bruce pick out for Carla."

"She isn't much on jewelry, so it was hard to find one that she would like. I personally fell in love with that one so suggested it."

Kevin stepped onto the stage from the wing opposite Jenna. He stopped when he saw her.

"Oh, there you are," Monica said. She waved him over with the hand holding the paint brush.

"I had to get a measuring tape." He held up the tape as he walked over.

"This is Jenna. She's the one looking into the note left for Bruce on the head table."

"Hi," Jenna said.

Kevin nodded then went over to a window and started taking measurements.

Jenna wasn't sure if he was rude, shy, or busy. She looked at Monica who gave a little shrug. She went back to her painting.

"I want to congratulate both of you on your engagement." Jenna checked Monica's ring finger. It was bare but that didn't mean anything. She was painting and probably took her it off so as not to get paint on it.

"Thank you," Monica smiled.

Kevin continued working. When he didn't answer, Monica prompted, "Right, Kevin?"

"Yes, thank you," Kevin mumbled.

"Kevin had asked me to marry him just before Bruce told me he wanted to propose to Carla. It was a pleasant surprise and that's what made me think of a double wedding."

"Do you think there'll still be a double wedding?"

"I don't know," Monica said, quietly. "They have more important things to think about now."

"Yes, I imagine setting a date is way down on their priorities. Are you and Kevin going to wait for them or continue with your own plans?"

"Oh, we're going to wait. Kevin knows how much it means to me." Monica spilled some paint on the floor and patted her pockets. "I have to go find a rag. I'll be right back." She went offstage.

Jenna watched Kevin mark his measurements on a piece of wood. She realized she didn't know anything about him other than his last name. She walked up to him.

"I saw you in the play," she said. "I thought you were really good."

"Thank you."

Not much of a conversationalist. "I'm a dating coach and I am always curious how people find each other in the big sea of humanity out there. How did you and Monica meet?" Carla had told her but she couldn't think of anything else to ask Kevin.

"We met when we both tried out for this play," Monica said, hurrying back on stage. "We kind of hit it off and have been seeing each other ever since. He's actually a very good actor."

"What do you do when not acting?" Jenna asked Kevin—she had to get him to say something more than 'thank you'.

"He's a financial advisor." Monica knelt down and wiped at the paint spill.

152

When Kevin didn't elaborate, Jenna returned to her seat. "To get back to the reason I am here. Any idea who threatened Bruce?"

"No, but then I don't know him well enough to know who might have a grudge against him from his past."

"So you think it has something to do with Bruce and isn't connected to the two deaths of Carla's previous fiancés?"

"One was murdered by a robber, the other died in an accidental fall. This is a threat, so that suggests to me it has to do with something else."

"Did you notice anything or anyone unusual that night?"

"I've thought about it but so far nothing has stood out about someone or something."

"What about you, Kevin?"

"No." He looked at his watch. "I have to go. I'll finish this tomorrow."

"Okay." Monica went up to him and hugged him. "I'll see you later, sweetheart."

Kevin wrapped his arms around her and gave her a peck on her cheek. "Sure."

"I've had a short conversation with Lillian and want to speak with Rachael," Jenna said, after Kevin had left. "Can you tell me anything about them?"

"Only that Lillian is our cousin and Rachael is an archaeologist and Carla's long-term friend. I met her when they were in high school together but once she started travelling, I seldom saw her. I think she's had the hots for Carla since they were teenagers."

"What?" Another bit of important news that hadn't been mentioned before.

Monica set the paint brush on the top of the can and stretched. "I know when we were teenagers, Rachael hung around a lot and always phoned Carla wanting to go to a movie together or shopping."

"That doesn't mean much. She could just have wanted a friend."

"True. But I'm sure there was more on Rachael's part."

"What about when they were adults?" Carla had never mentioned Rachael in all the years Jenna had known her.

"I didn't see Rachael once I left home and I'd thought she and Carla drifted apart when they became adults. I guess I was wrong because Rachael is one of her bridesmaids."

"Lillian was quite snappy when I talked with her and it seemed to me that Carla was abrupt with she spoke with Lillian the day after the engagement party. Did something happen between them at one time?"

"Well, they both fell in love with the same boy when they were in high school. I think Carla won him over by telling him that Lillian had herpes."

Now why hadn't either of them mentioned that? Jenna sighed. This was getting more complicated by the minute. "But that would have been years ago. Lillian would be over it by now."

"Oh, you don't know Lillian. When she was a teenager she didn't speak to her mother for a month because she wouldn't let her go to a party. She stalked a man where she worked for three months because he broke up with her. He finally got a restraining order against her and asked for a transfer to a different branch of the company."

Another bit of information withheld from her, Jenna thought. How did Carla expect her to find out the truth when she didn't tell her everything? Time to have a chat.

"Well, I hope this gets all straightened out so you and Carla can have the double wedding you want," Jenna said, standing.

"Yes, me too."

Jenna walked through the door into the foyer. A woman was wiping the bar counter. Jenna remembered her from the play.

"I saw you in the play Tuesday night. You were very funny."

The woman blushed. "Thank you. But it was just my character."

"I'm Jenna, a friend of Monica's."

"Beverley."

"Have you been acting long?"

"Actually, this is only the second play I've been in."

"Really?"

"Yes, and the reason I tried out for this part is because a man from work wanted to audition and he didn't want to go alone."

"Did you both get parts?"

"Yes, we did. But I knew Kevin would. He's been in a lot of plays. He eventually wants to get into television and movies."

"Kevin? Monica's fiancé?"

"Yes. We've worked at the same company for years."

"How long has he been acting?"

"Almost three years. Two years at another theatre and these few months of rehearsal here."

"And that's how he met Monica."

"Yes. How do you know Monica?"

"Her sister and I are friends."

"Oh. Carla. She's one of the producers for this play. A nice person."

"If Monica and Kevin only met at the beginning of rehearsals, it must have been a whirlwind romance. It sounds like the engagement was sudden."

"Well, it did surprise everyone in the play. I knew that they had been out a few times but I didn't know it had gotten that serious. They argue a lot about where they should stand and how they should deliver their lines during rehearsals."

"Oh?" Jenna said. That seemed a bit strange.

"And I don't know how long it will last."

"Why?"

"I saw Kevin get out of a car driven by another woman."

"Where and when was this?"

"Outside the theatre opening night."

"Did you recognize her? Could it have been a relative of his, like a sister?"

"I'd never seen her before. But he kissed her before getting out of the car."

"You're his friend. Is he a player?"

"Workmate, is more like it. And yes, he does flirt with the other women in the office. He really thinks he's a lady's man."

"Well, it was nice meeting you."

"You, too."

Jenna walked out of the theatre. She felt sorry for the sisters. Both of them were engaged to men who couldn't seem to be faithful.

Jenna went home and changed into her nightgown. She turned on the television to watch the news before going to bed. She liked to keep up with what was happening in the city, the country, and the world. Although most of it was disasters, diseases, and deaths, there were some heartwarming stories of people performing acts of kindness. She wished there were more feel-good stories but also knew it was human nature to want to know the details of dastardly deeds and disasters. She laughed out loud at her alliteration.

Jenna got herself an apple and settled on her couch. *Breaking News* flashed across the screen. She barely paid attention to those news flashes. Everything was considered breaking news nowadays.

"The partially decomposed body found near the Fraser River this past week has been identified as that of Gavin Hiscock. The coroner says he's been dead about seven months. The police are asking for anyone with any information about him to please come forward." The announcer then continued on to an accident on the Lougheed Highway that killed one person.

Jenna paused in her eating. So it was one of the brothers. Her thoughts turned to Drake. What was he going to do now? And Mrs. Hiscock. She could no longer hold on to the belief that the dead man was neither of her sons.

Jenna was startled by the ringing of her cell phone. She picked it up and saw Drake's name. She swiped to answer. "Hello?"

"Have you seen the news?"

"Yes, just now."

"I'm going to the police again tomorrow. I want to make sure that they check into the person named Trevor. Now that Gavin is dead, the fact that someone, who could have been him, wanted to tell me about his friend's brother is important."

Drake paused for a breath and Jenna heard the desperation in his voice when he continued. "I want to make sure the police haven't forgotten about Jonathon. I want them to keep his killing in mind when they are checking into Gavin's death."

"Did you find the paper with the phone number on it that I was given?"

"No, and I looked everywhere. I tried calling the number Mrs. Hiscock gave me, and like she said, it wasn't in service. That's probably because Gavin hasn't paid his bill for seven months."

Jenna had taken the next morning off because of a doctor's appointment. "Do you want me there with you? I could meet you about eleven."

"Thank you, but no. I just wanted to find out if you'd seen the news and tell you my plans."

"Well, let me know how it goes."

"I will."

CHAPTER 18

Carla sighed and stared down at the pen in her hand. She should have known this would come out. Nothing stayed a secret for long anymore. She looked up at Jenna sitting on the other side of her desk.

"Who told you?"

"Monica mentioned that Rachael had an attraction for you in high school. I was just wondering if anything developed between you, something that might make Rachael jealous of any man in your life."

"I knew Rachael was a lesbian when we were teenagers, but I thought she knew I was straight. I was so shocked when she tried to kiss me one night that I pushed her and told her I never wanted to see her again."

"And then what happened?"

"She stayed away from me for about six months. Then we met again at a mutual friend's party and she asked if I would let her back in my life again. I did miss the fun we'd had together, so I said yes. We were best friends again for the rest of high school."

"Monica thought you two hadn't seen much of each other as adults."

Carla felt herself blush. Should she tell the whole truth? "We were in and out of each other's lives over the years because of her travelling. I was feeling depressed after Dale and then Roger died and I was thinking I would never find a husband. I'd even decided to swear off men and marriage since they didn't seem to be for me. One day Rachael called and asked if I wanted to see a movie with her. We had a few drinks afterwards and ended up in bed together at her place. We had a short-term affair."

"Who ended it?"

"I did. After three months, I decided I wanted to get back in the heterosexual dating scene and that's when I came to you for help."

"Do you think she could have written the note to Bruce? Maybe she was hoping that if he left you, you would get back with her."

Carla thought back to one of hers and Rachael's conversations. "I don't know," she said. "I told her our relationship was just something I thought I needed at the time, but she said she could tell I had true feelings for her. When I told her it was really over, she kept showing up at my office, sending me flowers, asking me to lunch." Carla smiled ruefully. "She even asked me to marry her."

"How did Rachael react when you told her you were engaged?"

"She knew I was dating Bruce and she said she was glad for me. She happily accepted when I asked her to be my third bridesmaid."

"Have you told Bruce about your affair?"

"No. But I guess I should." Carla grimaced. "We did promise each other we wouldn't have secrets."

"I also found out last night that Monica and Kevin haven't been dating long."

"A few months. Why do you ask?"

"Some of the set builders and cast were working at the theatre last night with Monica. He was there and seemed very shy or standoffish. He hardly talked."

"Well, I really can't tell you much about him," Carla said. "A few months ago, Monica started talking about a man she was dating. But she never brought him around to meet mom or me. When I'd ask if she wanted to double date with Bruce and me, she'd always find an excuse. She had pictures of him with the cast which she showed us but that was all until she invited mom and me to lunch to meet him a few weeks ago."

"So, it's doubtful that he would have any resentment against Bruce or you."

"I can't think why he would. Like I said, I only met him a while ago. Bruce never said he knew him before."

"I've heard that you and Lillian liked the same boy when you were teenagers but you told him she had herpes."

Jeez, Jenna was certainly good a digging up the past. "Yes, that's true."

"Could she have held a grudge that long? Could this be her payback?"

"Oh, I highly doubt it. That's like over twenty-five years ago." Carla stopped. She didn't know for sure. "But I guess you would have to ask her that."

"One more question and it is really difficult. Feel free to kick me out of your office if you feel like it."

"Oh, this sounds a bit grim." Carla waited expectantly for the query.

"Did you write that note to get out of your upcoming wedding?"

Carla stared at Jenna. She couldn't believe that her friend had asked her that. After devoting her twenties and her early thirties to building her business to the detriment of everything else, she had been so delighted to find Dale and plan a future with him. She had been devastated when he was murdered and it had taken years for her to date again. Then Roger came into her life and she thought she had it all. After Roger's accident, she'd wondered if she would ever find happiness with another human being. Her fling with Rachael had been exciting and a novelty but that had quickly worn off. Thanks to Jenna, she'd found Bruce and she'd thought her life was finally complete. To even consider that she would do anything to jeopardize her wedding was unthinkable.

"No." Carla said, haughtily. She could think of no other words to get across the weight of her answer.

Jenna nodded. "I'm sorry, but I had to ask. And now, could Bruce have written the note for the same reason?"

"That, you will have to ask him."

*C*arla sat in the middle of the long table with Monica on one side and Becky in the wheelchair at the other. Becky's leg was elevated on the leg rest of the wheelchair and stuck out into the aisle between the tables. They were waiting for Roberta, Conrad, and Abigail to show up for their lunch date. She'd asked for a table for six when she'd phoned for a reservation. She thought it would best for her mother and would also be an easy escape if someone wanted to walk out.

The waitress came over with menus. "Would you like anything while you wait?"

"Just glasses of water for now," Carla said. "And make that six."

Becky looked at her watch. "They are already five minutes late," she said. "I wonder if they will show."

"Well, they'd better," Monica said. "I booked the afternoon off for this and to prepare for tonight's performance. So if they do come, I can't stay any longer than a couple of hours."

"There they are." Carla waved and watched as Roberta, Conrad, and Abigail came over. With Conrad and Abigail together, she could see a resemblance. Same shade of blond hair, same nose, same chin.

Roberta led the way. She was medium height with dyed black hair. She walked with determination. Conrad was tall like his father. His face had a permanent scowl to it. Abigail wore a knee-length skirt and matching jacket. She smiled as she approached the table. Roberta took the middle seat across from Carla. Conrad sat on her left across from Monica while Abigail sat in the remaining chair. The uncomfortable first few minutes of deciding what to say were forestalled by the waitress coming over with six glasses of water. She placed one in front of each of them.

"I'll come back in a while to take your orders."

"I know this is a bit awkward," Abigail said. "But thank you all for agreeing to come."

"Like we had a choice," Conrad snorted. "You kept begging until we gave in."

"And that's what big brothers are for," Abigail smiled sweetly at him.

Carla realized that this was a woman who was used to getting what she wanted. "Why did you want to meet?"

"Let's order first," Abigail said, opening her menu. "I'm hungry."

Carla felt a jolt of anger. Why was Abigail drawing this out? They could order after she had explained why she'd asked them to come. Carla certainly didn't expect this gathering was for everyone to forgive each other and live happily ever after as one big family and she wanted to get right to the reason. She looked around the table. Everyone was studying the menu in front of them. She reluctantly opened hers. She really didn't feel like eating, so ordered a salad when the waitress came over for their selections.

When the waitress left, Abigail took a manila envelope from her purse and handed it across to Becky. "Here are the results of my DNA tests that show I'm related to Conrad through our father."

Becky took a document out of the envelope and held it so Carla and Monica could look at it also. Carla scanned it, not understanding any of the explanations of the difference between the shared DNA between half-siblings and full-siblings, and the charts.

"Basically, it says Conrad and I are half-siblings," Abigail said. "I printed this copy off for you to read in-depth later."

"No thanks." Becky slid the document into the envelope and handed it to Abigail. "I'll take your word for it."

"As you please." Abigail returned the envelope to her purse.

"So, why are we here?" Carla asked, again.

"Well, I've never had a real family. It was always just my mom and me. When Mom was diagnosed with cancer and dying, I thought I was going to be alone forever. Then she told me about my father and that I had a half-brother. I found Conrad and we both took the DNA test. And now one half-brother has turned into two step-sisters and two step-mothers. I couldn't believe my luck." She stopped and looked around the table. "I just want to get to know all of you."

"But you have been told our history," Monica said. "We already know Roberta and Conrad and have no desire to have anything to do with them."

"And the feeling is mutual," Roberta added.

"But I think I've been sent to bring you all together; to unite you as one family. My family."

"That's not going to be possible," Carla said. She stood and picked up purse. "You are wasting your time."

"Please, please." Abigail held out her hand to Carla. "Please don't leave. Let's at least eat our lunch."

Carla glanced at her mother. It was her decision. Becky, in turn, looked at Roberta and Conrad. "I'm willing to stay if everyone promises to be civil."

"We've always been civil," Roberta said. "It's you who has caused all the trouble between us."

"Okay, we can leave," Becky said.

Carla went over to the wheelchair and jockeyed it around so she could push it away from the table. "I'll tell the waitress to cancel our three meals."

Monica also stood. "I would advise you to get over the joy of having a half-brother and look at them and their actions closely. They're not nice people."

"How dare you!" Roberta half-stood. "It wasn't me who stole someone's husband and then all his money so his first family didn't get anything!"

"See, first lie," Monica said. "They were left money in his will."

Carla pushed her mother to the front counter.

"Can you believe that?" Monica said, angrily. "They're still lying about us."

The waitress came over and Carla explained that they were leaving. She glanced back at the table to see the three in what appeared to be a heated argument. She guessed things had not gone as they had hoped.

"Can you take Mom outside?" Carla said to Monica. "I want to go ask them a question."

"About the note?" Monica asked, taking hold of the wheelchair handles.

"Yes. I want to see their reaction."

"Be careful," Becky said.

Carla walked back to the table. The arguing quit when they saw her.

"What do you want?" Conrad asked, irritably.

"Which one of you left it?" Carla asked.

"Left what?"

"The piece of paper."

"What piece of paper?" Roberta demanded.

"Yes, what are you talking about?" Abigail asked.

Carla looked at the three faces. They seemed genuinely puzzled. "Never mind." She turned to leave.

"Hey, what are you accusing us of now?" Conrad called, as she walked away.

"Did one of them leave it?" Monica asked when Carla joined them.

"I don't think so. They all seemed confused when I mentioned it."

"We didn't know Abigail at the time so she could have snuck into the party with it."

"Since meeting her, I've gone through all the photos Bruce and I received, looking specifically for her. I didn't find one and Bruce and I were able to account for everyone in the pictures as being on my side or his. With the number of pictures our family and friends have sent us, it would have taken a lot of luck for her or Roberta or Conrad to sneak in and not to be caught in a photo."

"So you are ruling them out as potential suspects," Monica said.

"Yes. And I'll let Jenna know."

"I'm still hungry," Becky said. "I feel like a pizza."

"There's a Pizza Parlour down the street." Carla pointed. "I can wheel you there."

"Let's go," Becky said. "I'm buying."

They reached the restaurant and Monica pushed the automatic opener switch. Carla guided the wheelchair through the doorway. They found a table and Monica moved two chairs aside so Carla could manoeuvre her mother sideways to the table.

"I think that was all a set-up," Becky said, when they'd ordered.

"What makes you say that?" Carla asked.

"The way Abigail tried to come across as so sweet, wanting a family. While I didn't have any interaction with her mother through the stores, I do know that Mary Spencer had two sisters and a brother who all lived in the greater Vancouver area. Mary told me about them at one of our parties. She said they always got together for holidays."

"You don't think she's Hayden's daughter?" Monica asked.

"Oh, I don't know about that, but I'm sure she was acting when she said she wanted us all to be one big happy family."

"So you think she believes their stories and therefore believes there is a lot of money and she is entitled to some of it?"

"That could be."

"What if she was hired to act the part of Hayden's daughter?" Carla asked. "Those papers looked quite technical and we only have her word that they are DNA tests."

"I guess I should have accepted them," Becky said.

"I doubt it would have done any good. If this was all a ruse, they would have made sure the bottom line of the papers showed Abigail and Conrad are related."

"Well, all three of them are certainly going to be shocked when my will is read and they find there is nothing to be divided up," Becky laughed.

CHAPTER 19

Jenna's phone rang as she pulled into her parking spot on Granville Island. She parked and removed it from her purse. "How did it go?" she asked Drake as she climbed out of her car.

"I talked with a Detective Wilson and told him the whole story about the hit-and-run driver killing Jonathon, the memorials Jonathon's parents have put on every year to raise money for Mothers Against Drunk Driving, and Gavin and Sean in the hospital with their spider tattoos. I told him about the man who approached me at the memorial last spring and gave me the name Trevor and the one who gave you the phone number. I told him everything and why I think they are all linked."

"And what did he say?"

"He wanted to know why after all these years the person would decide to talk to me. I told him I suspected that the person was Gavin and he may have been grateful to me for saving Sean's life. Wilson also wondered why the person would give you the phone number. Again, I could only guess that he'd seen us talking at the memorial after your 5K run."

Jenna entered the Net Loft and headed to the bookstore. "Is he going to do anything?"

"He said that it sounded like a lot of coincidences. I told him yes, but I think they add up to someone not liking that Gavin might have given me some information about the driver of the car that hit Jonathon. And that was it."

"What do you mean?"

Drake sighed, "The conversation was over. He thanked me and I left."

"So, it wasn't very productive." Jenna felt sorry for Drake. He was trying so hard to find justice for Jonathon and nothing seemed to be working.

"No. But I'll keep trying. Now tell me how your search for the note writer is going."

"Well, we're certainly uncovering a lot of secrets, but we haven't found anything that points to any one person."

They hung up and Jenna dialed Lillian's number. Might as well ask her about the herpes story right now.

"Hello."

"Lillian, its Jenna again."

"What do you want now?"

Jenna decided to ignore her rudeness. "I've heard that Carla told a boy you both liked that you had herpes."

Lillian laughed out loud and Jenna was surprised at how lighthearted and cheery it sounded. "That was so funny. He stayed six feet away from me when he asked me about it."

"So there was no animosity between you over it?"

"Well, at first, I was mad at her but then I realized she'd done me a favour. He only dated her a couple of times and then dumped her for a cheerleader." There was a pause. "And you called me because you're wondering if I've been angry at her all these years and scaring away her fiancé is my way of getting back at her."

"Something like that."

Lillian laughed again and Jenna liked the sound. Then the line went dead.

"I guess that was a 'no'," Jenna muttered as she walked into the bookstore. She was happy to see it full of customers. Both Adam and Michele were behind the tills and there was a line up at each one. It paid to have a once-monthly sale day. She stepped between the two and began bagging the sold books. When one o'clock came, Michele moved away from the till and Jenna took over.

"See you tomorrow," Jenna said.

"You bet," Michele smiled.

"How did your talk with Monica go last night?" Adam asked.

"It was an eye-opener." Jenna looked around to see if anyone was within hearing distance.

"It seems that Rachael is a lesbian and she liked Carla a lot when they were teenagers. I went to see Carla this morning and she told me they'd had a fling after Roger died, but she ended it and came to me to start dating men again."

"That certainly puts a new spin on things."

"Yes. Really makes you wonder if Rachael is trying to scare Bruce off so she and Carla could get back together. I phoned her and will be meeting her this evening."

Jenna went on to tell him the herpes story and Lillian's reaction to Jenna's phone call. "And Carla denied writing that note. I think she's not very pleased with me for asking."

"Did you ask if Bruce could have?"

"Yes and she told me to speak with him. So I'll ask him when we meet at the café here tomorrow. What about you? Anything new with you and Mason?"

"Unfortunately, no. But I also have a meeting tonight. I phoned Ronnie and I'm having drinks with him later. Maybe he can fill in some blanks on Bruce's love life."

"Oh, I almost forgot. It seems Kevin was seen kissing another woman."

"Great. Isn't anyone the person they appear to be?"

"It does seem that everyone has a secret. I wonder if we should talk with Kevin. Maybe he can give us an idea about what's happening." Jenna picked up her phone and stepped away from the cash register. She dialed Monica's number while Adam waited on a customer.

The phone rang.

"Hello?"

"Hi. Monica, Jenna here. I won't keep you long, because you are working but I'm wondering if you can give me Kevin's phone number."

"Why?"

"I'd like to ask him if he has remembered anything that was out of the ordinary, or someone he saw doing something that he now thinks was odd."

"He doesn't."

"Oh." Jenna was surprised. "I'd like to talk to him myself. Maybe a question I ask will jog his memory."

"We've talked about it. He doesn't remember anything unusual. You don't need to talk with him."

"Okay, thank you." Jenna tapped the red receiver to end the call.

"What?" Adam asked.

"She refused to give me his phone number."

"That's strange."

"That's what I thought. I wonder what she's hiding."

"Or he, or both of them."

"Yes. I think I'll talk with Carla about it." Jenna dialed Carla's number and waited while it rang three times.

"Hello?" Carla said, breathlessly.

"Carla, where did I get you from?"

"Oh, I had to go down the hall to see one of my designers. I heard my phone on my way back. What can I do for you?"

"I phoned Monica to ask for Kevin's number and she wouldn't give it to me."

"That's odd. Did she say why?"

"No. I thought you might know."

"Sorry, I haven't a clue."

"Do you happen to have his number?"

"Actually, no, I don't. I've never had a reason to ask for it."

"Okay, thank you. How was your lunch today?"

"You mean our almost lunch."

"Almost?"

"Abigail showed us the DNA test that confirmed she and Conrad were related, which Mom said she accepted as true. Then Abigail said she thought she'd been sent to bring us all together and she wanted us to work things out so she could have one big happy family."

"And it didn't go well."

"Not at all. Monica said we weren't interested and Roberta said the same. We were ready to leave, but Abigail begged us to at least stay for our lunch. Mom agreed but only if there was no fighting. Roberta said it wasn't them who were causing the trouble, so we left."

"That's too bad."

"Yes, but I've decided to rule them out as being the ones who put the note on the table. They seemed surprised when I asked about it and none of them have shown up in any pictures."

"Okay. We'll take them off our list."

Jenna hung up and put her phone in her purse. Time to get to work. The afternoon went fast and it wasn't long before she and

173

Adam were closing up. They carried the money trays to the office and Jenna sat in the chair with a sigh. It had been a long day. Adam pulled the other chair up to the opposite side of the desk and sat. They each counted out the floats and set them aside then began sorting and tallying the money as they talked.

Jenna glanced at the calendar on the desk where they wrote the activities scheduled for the month. "Tomorrow afternoon is the Children's Reading Hour and our monthly open mic is tomorrow evening."

"Yes, two more writers came in today to sign up for a reading."

"Good. That makes five. Plus the ones who show up for the two-minute speed reading. Do we know either of the new signees?"

"One of them is Sophia Bouvier."

"Sophia? Nice. I wonder if she is going to read from the mystery novel she and her sister are writing."

Adam handed his tray with its float and the deposit bag to Jenna. She put them and her tray in the safe behind the desk. There wasn't a bank on Granville Island, only ATM machines. Because she had a car, Jenna usually went to their bank on Broadway to make a deposit on her way home in the evening. Tonight, with both of them going out, they decided to leave the money until tomorrow.

Jenna shut off the lights and they locked up the bookstore. "Where are you meeting Ronnie?"

"Just at The Keg here. What about you?"

"I'm off to the Cactus Club on Burrard."

"Oh, fancy."

They walked together down the darkened street. Suddenly, they heard tires squealing. Jenna and Adam turned in time to see headlights coming at them.

"What the hell?" Adam shouted, as they both jumped behind one of the cement parking barriers.

A dark car sped past them. Jenna tried to see the license plate.

"Stupid idiot!" Adam yelled at the taillights. "Why are people in such a hurry at night?"

"I'm not sure if it was random," Jenna said.

"What do you mean?"

"It looked like someone deliberately put something over the license plate so I couldn't read it."

"You mean the driver tried to run us down? Who would want to do that?"

"I'm not saying that. It's just suspicious."

"Well, be careful."

"You, too."

*J*enna parked on the street near the Cactus Club and walked in. She checked for the woman she had only seen on the night of the engagement party. She tried to remember what she looked like.

"I'm meeting someone," Jenna told her hostess.

"What's their name?"

"Rachael." Jenna realized she didn't know Rachael's last name.

"Follow me."

The hostess led Jenna through the restaurant to a booth in the far corner. Jenna recognized the woman who appeared to be in her early forties. The slacks and jacket were certainly different from the fancy mauve dress and matching heels. Her hair was in a ponytail, not styled.

"Hi, Rachael. I'm Jenna"

"Nice to meet you." Rachael waved at the bench seat across from her. "Please, sit."

"Thank you for agreeing to see me," Jenna said as she took off her coat and sat on the seat. She put her coat and purse beside her.

"Well, we have to find out who is threatening Bruce, don't we."

"Yes." Jenna agreed.

A server came over and placed glasses of water in front of them. "Would you like anything else to drink?"

"The water is fine," Jenna said and Rachael nodded. "I also know what I want to eat," Jenna added.

"Me, too," Rachael said.

Jenna ordered salmon aburi roll while Rachael asked for the crab cakes.

After the server left, Jenna wondered when she should ask the important question. *Not right off,* she decided. "You and Carla have been friends for a long time."

"Yes."

"How did you meet?"

"We first met playing soccer in middle school and then since we both liked writing we worked on our school paper in high school."

Jenna wasn't sure how to approach the subject about Rachael's relationship with Carla. "I'm wondering if you noticed anyone place that note under Bruce's plate."

"No, but then I didn't hang around the table that much."

Jenna tried to remember if she'd seen Rachael on the dance floor but couldn't. There always seemed to be a crowd while the band played.

"I've heard you and Carla had an affair last year." Jenna watched her reaction.

Rachael sat back in the booth. "How did you find out?"

"Carla."

Rachael looked surprised. "She admitted it?"

"Yes."

"Did she sound happy that we'd been together or wistful that we split up?"

Jenna didn't know how to answer that. It was obvious that Rachael still had feelings for Carla.

"Oh, I get it," Rachael said. "Because I had an affair with Carla and didn't like it when she broke up with me, I'm one of the suspects."

"I wouldn't say 'suspects', but everyone at the head table had a better chance of doing it than anyone else."

"You're right, but it wasn't me. Yes, I love Carla, and yes I'd like to get back together with her, but I would never threaten anyone like that."

"You've had feelings for her since you were teenagers."

"Ah, she told you the story of our first kiss," Rachael laughed. "I was just acknowledging to myself that I was a lesbian and exploring my feelings. We spent a lot of time together so I wondered if Carla was also going through the same introspection. It turned out I was wrong and it almost cost me her friendship.

"I was so happy when we met at the party and our friendship was renewed. As we got older, I realized that what I felt for her was love but I kept it to myself. You can't imagine my delight when we started our affair." She paused. "I … I thought we would be together forever." She sighed. "But I was wrong."

Jenna's phone rang as she climbed into her car after saying goodbye to Rachael. She saw it was Drake. She hoped he had some good news.

"Hi. Drake."

"Jenna, can you meet me at the Earl's on Broadway in half an hour?" Drake asked breathlessly.

"Sure, what's happening?" She was alarmed. "Is something wrong?"

"Mrs. Hiscock phoned and wants to meet us. She said it's urgent."

"Okay, I'll be right there." Jenna hung up.

*A*dam tried to picture what Ronnie looked like as he walked into the Keg. He'd only seen him at the engagement party when Ronnie had given a short speech about himself and the groomsmen. He remembered a tall slim man with short brown hair. And that described about half the male population. He stood inside the door and scanned the room.

"May I help you?" the woman behind the counter asked.

"I'm supposed to meet someone," Adam said.

"There is a gentleman sitting in that booth who said he was waiting for a guest." She pointed towards one halfway down the aisle.

"Thank you." Adam walked in that direction hoping he would recognize Ronnie. But he didn't have to worry. He saw Ronnie wave at him.

Adam smiled as he slid into the seat across from Ronnie. "I don't know how you realized that I'm Adam."

"I saw you with Mason at the party." Ronnie pointed to the menu in front of Adam. "The server will be here soon so let's order and then we can discuss my ideas on who I think left the note for Bruce."

Adam opened the menu in front of him. He scanned it and settled on a burger and fries while Ronnie ordered the blackened chicken. They both asked for water as a drink.

"Okay, so tell me your ideas on the note." Apparently, Ronnie didn't care for small talk.

"Well, to begin with: the maid of honour. I've met Monica a few times since Bruce and Carla began dating. She seems quite intense and driven and she seldom smiles. I only met Lillian two weeks ago when Bruce and Carla brought most of us together to discuss how the engagement evening would go. And I was introduced to Rachael on the day of the party. So I really can't speak to motives any of them might have."

Ronnie paused to take a drink of water. "As you know from my speech, Bruce, Bill, and I have been friends for decades. Mason wanted to be part of our group and always hung around when his family visited Bruce's family. He really was a pain in the butt, always whining that he would tell Bruce's parents if we didn't include him in our activities. I didn't like him then, and I still don't now. Even though he's a grown man I haven't gotten over that crybaby spoiling our fun."

So far, Ronnie hadn't said anything that Adam didn't already know. "Of all the people at the table, who do you think would have left the note?"

"Well, because I know it wasn't Bill or me, or Bruce for that matter, it either had to be Mason or one of the women."

"Do you have any proof? Did you see any of them acting suspicious?"

"I know you and Carla's friend, Jenna, are trying to solve this mystery and I'm sorry to disappoint you, but that's just my opinion. I never saw anything remarkable and I can't point a finger at anyone in particular."

Their meals arrived and Adam dug into his burger. He was disheartened. Everyone seemed to have stories from the past that gave possible motives but no one they had talked with so far had any real evidence against anyone else. They all seemed to be standing together. Was this like the story in Agatha Christie's mystery novel, *Murder on the Orient Express*? Were all the men trying to stop Bruce from marrying Carla? Did Monica, Rachael, and Lillian think Bruce wasn't good enough for Carla? Or were all six of them in this together? Had they ganged up against the future bride and groom? Adam mentally shook his head. What an absurd thought. Maybe it was time for small talk.

"Do you have any children?" That was safe and usually got parents talking or showing photographs.

"No children and never been married."

Okay, that was a short conversation. Adam did have one more question and he wasn't sure how to ask it. It was personal and had nothing to do with the mystery of the note.

"Mason told me he has a sister but it was Bruce who said her name is Destiny and she disappeared years ago. I'm wondering if there is anything I should know about it so I don't make a blunder and say something inappropriate when I'm with Mason."

Ronnie coughed into his napkin and took a few moments before answering. "That's a name I haven't heard in a long time. It surprised me." He was quiet again. "I don't think there is anything that you could say that would upset Mason. At the time, we all heard the theories that she was abducted and murdered or that she ran away. Someone even suggested that she might have been in an accident and had amnesia. But as you know, nothing has ever been proven."

Ronnie's answer told him nothing. "Anything else? Does the family or police know who the guy was she was supposed to be meeting?"

"Not that I've heard. We were all questioned because of Bruce being family, and Bill and I knowing her."

"Did you date her?"

"Destiny was a beautiful girl. Bill dated her for a while and when they broke up I asked her out. We went to the movies a few times and double dated with Bruce and his girlfriend at the time but Destiny and I had nothing in common and we quit seeing each other. I have no idea what happened to her and as far as I know, her disappearance has no relevance to the note."

Funny, that was almost the same statement as Bruce's when he was asked about Destiny. Neither one of them seemed to want to talk about her.

Adam was out of questions and they had finished eating. There was no use sticking around. He signaled for the bill. "Thank you for meeting me."

"I just wish I had something more to tell you," Ronnie said. "I hate to think that someone might actually kill Bruce if he continues with the wedding."

CHAPTER 20

*J*t was dark and raining as Jenna drove to Earl's, but luckily it wasn't that far and the traffic was light. She was there fifteen minutes after speaking with Drake. His car was already in the lot and she parked beside it. She didn't know what type of vehicle Mrs. Hiscock drove so she couldn't tell if she'd arrived. Jenna entered the restaurant and just pointed to Drake when the hostess came over. The hostess smiled and nodded. Drake was looking out the window at the parking lot.

"Hi," Jenna said, sitting down.

Drake smiled at her and then went back to watching the cars entering and leaving the lot. He had a glass of water in front of him.

"I'll have an orange juice," Jenna told the waitress.

"There she is," Drake said, eagerly. "And I think that's her son, Sean, with her."

Jenna saw a woman and a man crossing the barely lit lot. She squinted but couldn't make out what Sean looked like. They both turned to the door and watched as the two entered. Mrs. Hiscock stopped and surveyed the room. Drake waved and stood as they approached. Sean was different than Jenna expected. She knew he was in his teens, but he carried himself like a much more mature man. He was slim and dressed in blue jeans and a black jacket. His dark hair was slicked back and in a ponytail. She could make out part of the tattoo on his neck.

"Hello, Mrs. Hiscock," Drake said. He turned to her son and held out his hand. "Sean. It's good to see you again."

Sean shook his hand. "Doctor Ferrell."

"And this is my friend, Jenna."

Jenna nodded at him.

"First of all, I apologize for my abruptness at our last meeting," Mrs. Hiscock said, as they sat down. "You don't know the fear we've lived with over the past few months. And then you start asking questions about Gavin and Sean. It really scared me."

They were quiet as the waitress came over. Mrs. Hiscock ordered a coffee while Sean asked for a pop.

"So why did you contact me now?" Drake asked when she had left.

"It was Sean's idea. I'll let him tell you."

Sean looked down at his hands, then up at Drake. "I was stupid last spring trying heroin at my birthday party. I was lucky my friends got me to the emergency room in time for you to give me the Naloxone. You saved my life."

"It's my job," Drake smiled.

"Gavin was so mad at me for being stupid. When he realized it was your nephew who was being remembered at the memorial that was on the news and you'd been looking after him when he died, he decided he had to do something for you. A couple of years ago, while they were drinking at a party, one of his friends told him that his brother had been the driver of the red sports car that killed the little boy years before. Gavin hadn't believed him because the brother would have been only fourteen at the time."

The waitress returned with their drinks and Sean immediately took a gulp. "After you saved my life, Gavin asked his friend if the story he'd told him was true and his friend told him to shut up and never mention it again. Gavin told me about it and said he was going to give you the kid's name so you could take it to the police."

"But he didn't show up for our meeting. I tried calling his number but he never answered."

"And we had't seen him since, either," Mrs. Hiscock said. "But he did phone me that day, probably about the same time he was at the fair, and told me to hide Sean. He said he was going to do something that could put both their lives in danger. I asked him what was happening but he said he could handle it."

"Oh," Drake said. "That would have been frightening."

"It was."

"Did you go to the police?" Jenna asked.

"No," Mrs. Hiscock shook her head. "We really had nothing to tell them. Gavin hadn't said the boy's name and he was old enough to go wherever he wanted and for all we knew that's what he'd done." She looked at Sean. "Sean's father and I decided to send him to my sister's place in Nova Scotia. We've been praying ever since that Gavin would show up and say he'd gone on a long holiday, but he never did, until last week." She picked up a napkin from the table and dabbed her eyes.

"I just got back today," Sean said.

"Did you remember anything about the Trevor Gavin mentioned. His last name or anything about him?" Jenna asked, looking from Sean to his mother.

"When Gavin's body was discovered I looked through a bunch of boxes in our attic," Mrs. Hiscock said. "Some were from when Gavin's mother still lived there. I found some of Gavin's school yearbooks and scanned through them. I found three boys with the name Trevor. I wrote them down."

She dug a piece of paper from her purse. She handed it to Drake. Jenna looked over his shoulder at the three names: Trevor Banyon, Trevor Smith, and Trevor Mayler.

"Do you remember any of them?" Drake asked.

"No."

"Why are you coming to us? You should be going to the police with this."

"Oh, we are," Mrs. Hiscock said. "We just want both of you with us because this whole thing involves your nephew, and you have the information to fill in the gaps in what we know. Will you come?"

"Yes, of course," Drake said.

"Definitely," Jenna said. She would do anything to finally give Drake the peace he needed.

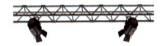

*A*dam entered his condo and closed the door. His meeting with Ronnie hadn't been very productive but during their conversation he'd come up with a theory about who may have threatened Bruce. He wanted some confirmation that it could be possible before he mentioned it to Jenna.

He removed his jacket and got himself an iced tea. He turned on his computer and typed in 'Black Widow'. Up came a movie starring Scarlett Johansson. Not what he was looking for. He tried a different website and it was about a 1987 movie starring Debra Winger.

Okay. Try something else.

He typed in 'Black Widow murderers' and smiled when a 2016 *Rolling Stone* article with the title *Killer Wives: 8 Most Infamous Black Widow Murderers* opened onto his screen. This was what he wanted and he began reading.

The term 'black widow' was taken from the female black widow spider that eats the male spider after they've had sex. The name was given to women who kill their partners. It seemed that female killers usually murdered the men closest to them for financial gain or to get back at abusive husbands, or just because they wanted to. He read the story about Canadian Evelyn Dick who was called the 'Torso Killer' for killing and dismembering her husband, John, in 1946 after only six months of marriage. Her father and one of her boyfriends helped with the cutting up of his body.

Her father burned the limbs in his furnace and they threw the torso away in the woods. While her father was charged and found guilty of being an accessory after the fact, Evelyn was found guilty of the murder and then, on appeal, was acquitted on a technicality. However, she was found guilty of killing her own infant son whose mummified body was found in her attic. She served eleven years and was released, given a new identity, and disappeared from public.

"I wonder if she was still alive when I was growing up in Ottawa. What if she moved to the city and was one of my neighbours? What if she was old lady Bradbury?"

Adam thought of the old woman down the block who didn't have any family and never had visitors. He and his friends used to walk past her house on their way to school. Occasionally, they'd see her tending the flowers in her front yard. He didn't know what she did in her back yard.

Adam continued reading about Mary Elizabeth Wilson, a British woman who, after losing four husbands between 1955 and 1957, was known as the 'Merry Widow of Windy Nook'. Fortunately, she was married to them long enough to inherit their estates. When the police exhumed the bodies, it was found that they all had ingested insecticide. Mary was sentenced to death in 1958 and was almost the last woman to be hanged in England. However, her sentence was reduced to life imprisonment. She died in 1963 at aged 70.

Adam laughed at the last couple of sentences in the article. *Mary was known for her dark humour. At one of her wedding receptions, she was asked what to do with the left-over sandwiches and cakes. Supposedly she answered, "We'll keep them for the funeral."*

Adam read about the black widow of Kyoto who collected seven million dollars in insurance money from the deaths of seven men she dated between 1994 and 2013, and Kelly Cochran who got her husband to help her kill her boyfriend in 2014. They chopped him up and friends claim they served some of his body pieces to them at a barbeque. She then murdered her husband in 2016 and was eventually found guilty of both murders.

Adam typed in 'women killers' and one of the stories he found dated back to 1916 and was about Amy Archer-Gilligan, who ran a nursing home. Most of her clients were elderly and sick and many died while in her care. Luckily for her, many of them had just named her their beneficiary on their insurance policies or had given her a sizable amount of money to pay for their future care. Over five years, from 1911 to 1916, forty-eight people died in her nursing home.

Amy's husband, who had a generous life insurance, also died. Eventually, someone became suspicious and went to the police. Each body they exhumed had traces of arsenic in it, and Amy was charged with poisoning five people. Her lawyer got the charge reduced to one murder. She was found guilty and given a life sentence. She died in 1962 at the age of 94. Her story was made into a play and then into the 1944 movie, *Arsenic and Old Lace,* which starred Cary Grant.

"One of my favourite old black and white movies," Adam mused.

Adam shut off his computer and stood. He'd found out more about black widows murderers than he'd expected but it all supported his idea on who may have written that note. Now, all he had to do was convince Jenna that it was a possibility.

CHAPTER 21

*T*he next morning, Adam and Jenna waited behind the counter ready to serve the customers who were wandering around the store. Adam listened as Jenna told him about her supper with Rachael.

"Poor woman," Adam said. "It's tough loving someone who doesn't return the emotion."

"Yes, she did seem broken-hearted when she told me," Jenna said. "I think she would take Carla back in a minute if Carla was willing."

"Which brings me to some research I did last night on women killers," Adam said, pleased with his segue. "In the 1950s and 60s, a woman named Jean Sinclair ran a nursing home. She fell in love with LaRae Peterson, the hairdresser at the home, and they had an affair. However, LaRae's sexuality was more fluid and she started dating a man named Don Foster. Jean tried to get LaRae back and when she wouldn't return, Jean shot and killed Don."

"Where did you get that story?"

"On the Internet. But it does show that Rachael could have killed Dale and Roger in order to stop Carla from marrying them. She must have been so happy when Carla turned to her after Roger's death and devastated when Carla ended the affair. Now she's out to get Bruce."

"Well, according to her, she isn't, but we won't rule her out. So what did Ronnie have to say last night?"

"Not much. He doesn't like Mason, hasn't since they were children, so the feeling is mutual between them. He has no idea who would have left the note."

"I was afraid of that. They all claim to know nothing."

"That's what I thought. I even wondered if it was a version of *Murder on the Orient Express* only they have banded together to stop the wedding. I also asked Ronnie about Mason's sister, Destiny. I wanted to find out enough so that I didn't make a faux pas if I mention her to Mason."

"What did he say?"

"He seemed surprised when I mentioned her and said it was a name he hadn't heard in a long time. Both he and Bill dated Destiny, Bill first. Ronnie and Destiny double-dated a couple of times with Bruce and his girlfriend but eventually split because they had nothing in common. Ronnie has no idea what happened to her and as far as he knows, her disappearance has no relevance to the note. Basically the same thing Bruce said when we asked him about her."

"Strange. Did you learn anything else, like, is he married, engaged, is he moving to Whistler when the business is in operation?"

"I didn't think to ask the other questions but he isn't married."

"Oh?" Jenna raised one eyebrow.

"No," Adam laughed. "He's not a friend of Dorothy's. And stop trying to be a matchmaker."

Jenna stuck her tongue out. "It's one of my jobs, remember? Have you been able to speak with Bill?"

"I've left two messages on his phone but so far he hasn't called me back." Adam took out his cell phone to check. "No, still nothing."

"That seems a little suspicious. He knows we're checking into the note. You'd think he would be eager to help his friend find out who'd threatened him."

"We might have to get Bruce to call him."

"I think one of us should talk with Ronnie's cousin about the affair she and Bruce had after Bruce was engaged," Jenna said. "Did Mason give you a last name?"

"I'll send him a text and find out."

Two customers came up to the counter at the same time. "Can you tell me more about this open mic tonight?" one asked Jenna.

While Jenna took her aside to explain how an open mic evening worked, Adam put his cell phone in his pocket and smiled at the second customer. "Did you find everything you were looking for?"

"Well, not really. I want to buy a new release but I see you don't have it."

"What is the name and I can order it for you."

"*Think About That* by Dick Sheldon."

Adam wrote that down. "And your name and phone number."

"Bobbi with an *i*, and 555-733-8181."

"Okay Bobbi. I'll send out the order today and call you when it comes in."

Adam felt his phone vibrate and looked at it as Jenna came back. "Her name is Linda Brown," Adam told her, quietly. "He sent her phone number. I'll give her a call as soon as I serve this lady coming up." Again, Adam put his cell away as he watched a woman approach the counter.

"Which book would you recommend for a three-year-old?" the woman asked, holding up three children's books for Adam to see. "She likes me to read to her."

"Well, if she likes animals, then she would enjoy *Lucky Lucky Ducky* or *Rascal, the Amazing Donkey*. If she likes the outdoors then *Learning Through Doing* will show her what to watch for on a walk in the woods. If she is creative then *Making Up Time* will teach her how to make up a story."

"Oh, they all sound good. And my granddaughter does like animals, going for walks with me, and telling me stories, so I guess I have to buy them all."

"Good choice," Adam smiled. "You'll be her favourite grandmother." He rang up the sale and bagged the books. He then walked away from the counter and dialed Linda's number while Jenna helped another customer.

"Hello, Linda? My name is Adam and I'm a friend of Bruce's."

"Ah, the amateur sleuth who's going to solve the mystery of who left a note on the head table. Ronnie told me *all* about you. What do you want to know?"

"Well, I don't have time to talk right now but could we get together soon?"

"I'm free tonight."

"Oh, that's not going to work. I co-own a bookstore and we are having an open mic tonight for authors to come and read some of their writing."

"An open mic? Can anyone come?"

"Yes."

"Well, I write poetry so I can show up and do a reading and then we can talk afterwards."

"Perfect. It's the Novel Bookshop in the Net Loft on Granville Island. We start at five-thirty."

"What did she say?" Jenna asked, when Adam came back.

"She said Ronnie told her about us checking into who would have threatened Bruce. She's coming to the open mic and reading some of her poetry."

"Nice. It's been a while since we've had a poet do a reading."

"Hopefully she can shed some light on what's happening."

"Yes," Jenna said. "I'm starting to feel guilty that it's been a week and we still have no idea who was behind the note."

"But nothing has happened to Bruce in that time so maybe it was just a joke. Someone who knew about Carla's past fiancés and was pranking him."

"That's a terrible prank to pull. And if it were a friend of mine, we wouldn't be friends anymore."

"So far, everyone we've talked with has denied any knowledge of the note and never saw anyone who might have left it," Adam said. "And we have no way of checking to see if any of them is lying. So let's go over what we've learned. Maybe something will jump out at us."

"Okay," Jenna agreed. "In no particular order, Bruce had a fling with Linda after becoming engaged to Carla. From Carla's reaction when we asked Bruce if he had any exes who might want him back, I think she knows about it."

"Or maybe that was because she has an ex-girlfriend that she's kept quiet about," Adam pointed out.

"Oh." Jenna nodded. "I never thought about it but you might be right."

"Two is the relationship Carla had with Rachael before meeting Bruce. What if Bruce found out about it and wanted to call the wedding off?"

"I wonder how I can bring that up at our lunch today. Carla did say she was going to tell him but she didn't say when."

"Three," Adam said. "Monica has a whirlwind romance and suddenly becomes engaged just before Carla and Bruce. Her fiancé seems to be a player."

"And according to the woman I spoke with at the theatre, they fight a lot. In fact, I overheard them arguing at the engagement party. Kevin wanted to leave early and Monica told him that as her fiancé he had to stay."

"Four, Ronnie wrecked Bruce's motorcycle years ago which caused a rift in their friendship for a while. Five, Rachael is still in love with Carla and would like to get back together—something Carla is against. Six, until the wedding Mason stands to inherit Bruce's money and seems to be a little short of cash."

"And don't forget about Bill's Facebook post," Jenna said.

"Right," Adam agreed. "Although, that's probably a bust. So far nothing more has happened there."

"Jeez, not much to go on after a week," Jenna said, disappointed.

"No, and we haven't even started speaking with the people who attended the party."

"Oh, I'm not even going to attempt that." Jenna shook her head. "Neither Carla nor Bruce can think of anyone they invited who would do such a thing so I'm taking their word on it."

"Nothing has shown up in the photos so they seem to be a dead end."

"Yes, the only one that had promise was blurry and the woman unidentifiable."

Adam didn't know what to say next. It had seemed an easy quest last week. Ask a few questions, find the culprit, and get them to confess all in an hour like they do on television. Now after seven days, while they knew nothing more about the note, they sure did know a lot more about the people involved. Everyone had some sort of skeleton in their closet.

The door opened and Carla rushed in, Monica close behind her. They both had a wild expression on their faces and they looked as if they hadn't slept.

"Carla, what's the matter?" Jenna asked.

"Jenna." Carla leaned on the counter. "Someone tried to run over Kevin last night."

"What? Where? Is he okay?"

"He has a concussion, broken wrist, and some cuts and bruises. The doctor is keeping him in the hospital for observation."

Jenna looked at Monica. "Were you with him?"

"No, luckily. He'd left the theatre before me."

"Come and sit down," Adam said. "You both look like you need a cup of tea."

"A good stiff drink would be better," Carla said, as she and Monica came around the end of the counter.

"Sorry, all we have is tea or coffee." Jenna guided Carla to one of the stools while Adam helped Monica.

"Coffee for me," Monica said. "We've been at the hospital all night."

"Tea would be nice," Carla said.

"I'll be right back." Adam hurried away.

"So tell me what happened," Jenna said. She was glad there were no customers and for the first time since they'd open the store, she hoped no one would come in for a while. This was serious.

"I don't know for sure," Monica said. "We put on our show and when it was over, everyone took off their costumes and removed their make-up as usual. They straggled out of the theatre to go home. Kevin was leaving before me since he had to be up early this morning for a golf game."

"Golf game in October?" Jenna asked.

"He and some of his friends are golf fanatics and they try to play all year round. Sometimes, if the weather is bad here, they'll go to any course that's open on Vancouver Island."

"So, he left before you. What happened next?"

"Well, when I was finished I went out to my car. I heard groaning and looked around. I was surprised to see his car was still parked. I found him on the ground beside it. I called 911 for an ambulance and the police."

"Was he able to tell you anything?"

"Just that he was halfway across the parking lot when he heard a car revving, and then tires squealing. He turned in time to see headlights coming at him. He threw himself out of the way and must have knocked himself out. When he woke up, his head and wrist hurt. He was trying to sit up when I found him."

"Did he get a look at the car or driver?" Jenna thought about the vehicle that had come close to hitting her and Adam the evening before. Were they related? Should she mention it? Maybe not now. Carla and Monica had enough to think about.

Monica shook her head. "He told the police that he was so intent on getting out of the way that he didn't see much. He thought the car was a dark colour but had no idea of the make or model and he didn't see who was inside."

Jenna looked at the sisters. This was not good. Someone left Carla's fiancé a threatening note and now someone had tried to kill Monica's fiancé. Was it the same person? Who disliked them bad enough to do that?

Adam came back with a tray. He handed Carla and Monica each a cup while Jenna filled him in on what she'd learned.

"There's coffee creamer and sugar on the tray if you want them," Adam said. "Does Kevin think the person was trying to kill him or just scare him?"

"What do you mean?" Monica asked, taking a sip of her coffee.

"Did the car actually hit him?"

"No. He jumped out of the way before it could. Oh," Monica gasped. She looked wide-eyed at Carla. "Do you think this could be related to Bruce's note?"

"I don't know." Carla shook her head. "It doesn't seem likely."

"But what if someone is trying to scare both of our fiancés? Someone who doesn't want either of us to marry."

"Who would want to do that to us?" Carla asked.

"I know you ruled out Roberta and Conrad, but they're the only two who would have it in for both of us," Monica said.

"What do you think, Jenna?" Carla asked.

"It does give us something more to consider."

"Like what?"

"Like maybe Monica or Kevin is the target instead of you or Bruce," Jenna said, thinking of the woman Kevin was seen kissing. "The note was just a smokescreen."

Everyone was quiet while they digested that.

"But I don't know anyone who would want to hurt Kevin or me," Monica said.

"What do you know about Kevin's past?' Adam asked. "It sounds like you two hadn't been dating long before getting engaged."

"I know he's a nice guy and he loves me."

"Does he have an ex-wife, ex-girlfriends who might not like him getting married again?"

"He was married for eight years and he and his ex-wife have a daughter together. They've been divorced for two years and she's remarried. He's had girlfriends but he said those relationships ended amicably."

"What hospital is he in?" Jenna asked. "Would we be able to go talk with him?" She remembered how abrupt Monica had been when she'd asked for his phone number.

"No. He's not allowed visitors."

"Okay." Jenna said, slowly.

"And he has nothing to add to what I've told you." Monica turned to Carla. "I think we should go. I need some sleep before our performance tonight."

"Will your play still be able to go on tonight without Kevin?" Adam asked.

"Oh, yes. There are understudies who learn a number of parts just in case someone gets sick or hurt."

Jenna watched Carla and Monica pet Maggie on the head as they left the store. There was something about the conversation that bothered her.

"What?" Adam asked.

"Hmm?"

"I know that look. Your mind is up to something."

"I don't know. How did Monica seem to you?"

"Well, I got the impression Carla was more upset than she was."

"Yes, I did too." Jenna said. "Anything else?"

"She still doesn't want us to talk with Kevin."

"Did Carla seem surprised when Monica said Kevin wasn't allowed visitors?"

"You noticed that, too." Adam nodded.

"I wonder what it all means. Do you suppose there could be a connection with the car that sped past us a few nights ago?"

"Oh, I hadn't thought about it. If there is then things are getting scary. The person's actions are escalating."

The bell jangled over the door and three women and a young girl entered.

"Good morning," Jenna said.

The women smiled while the little girl headed to the children's section.

Jenna turned back to Adam. "What do you think of the idea of someone being after Monica and Kevin instead of Bruce and Carla?"

"Why was the note threatening Bruce, then?"

Jenna shook her head. "Maybe they are two separate incidences. If that's true, then those women sure are having bad luck." She looked thoughtful. "You know, Monica never said what hospital Kevin was in."

Adam picked up his phone and looked up a number. He dialed it. While he waited, he took out a pen and paper from under the counter.

"Hello, I'm phoning to find out what room Kevin Barkley is in." He listened. "Okay, thank you." He looked at Jenna. "He's not at Vancouver General."

He looked up another number and asked the same question. He wrote something down and then asked what visiting hours were. "He's in the men's ward at St. Paul's Hospital."

"Nicely done," Jenna smiled. "I wonder if we should try and sneak in to talk with him. Find out about his engagement to Monica."

"Well, they're open around the clock for visiting. We can go after talking with Linda tonight."

CHAPTER 22

*J*enna saw that it was almost one o'clock, time for Children's Reading Hour, and there were already two boys, four girls, and two adults in the Children's Corner. She went to the children's section and pulled out two picture books. One was a new Hallowe'en story that had arrived last week and the other was about bats.

"Good morning, everyone," she said, sitting in the storyteller's chair. She smiled at the expectant faces of the children sprawled on the floor.

"Good morning," the children answered, enthusiastically.

"Today I will be reading *The Scariest Night of the Year*. Do you know what night that is?"

"Hallowe'en!" they all shouted.

At one time, Jenna had tried to keep the children quiet so as not to disturb the customers. Then she had decided the reading hour should be a time of fun for them and had let them display their natural enthusiasm.

"How many more days until Hallowe'en?"

There was a moment's quiet then one girl answered, "Ten."

"Right you are, Millie. And how many of you have your costumes ready?"

A number of hands shot up in the air.

"I'm going as a wizard," Scott said.

"And I'm going as Anna from the movie *Frozen*," Bree added.

"That's wonderful," Jenna said. She held up the book with a colourful picture of a witch and four children riding a long broom. They were flying over False Creek in Vancouver. She opened it and held it so the children could see the pictures as she read.

When the story time was over, **Jenna went to the counter where she sold seven copies of** *The Scariest Night of the Year*. One thing about Children's Reading Hour, it did increase sales of the books she read. She looked at her watch. She and Bruce had agreed to meet at two. It was time to go. She said goodbye to Adam and went to the café to get a table for her and Bruce.

She watched for him and waved when he walked in. He smiled and hurried over. Jenna noticed a few women turn as he passed their tables. He was tall and handsome in a George Clooney sort of way and she could understand why Carla or any woman found him attractive. While Bruce held the table for them, Jenna went for sandwiches at the counter and also brought back a cup of coffee for him and a bottle of orange juice for herself.

"Thank you for meeting me," Jenna said.

"Well, you did say it was important that we talk alone. Have you found out something you don't want Carla to hear?"

That was such a big opening, but not one Jenna wanted to enter at the beginning of their conversation. There were other things she hoped to learn before possibly making Bruce mad enough to storm out.

"We haven't been able to get a hold of Bill," Jenna led out with. "Do you know why he isn't returning our calls?"

"He's out of town on business."

"Oh, what does he do?"

"He's a salesman for a pharmaceutical company."

So he might have left the note knowing he would be gone for a while. That could explain why nothing new had happened since last Saturday, unless you counted someone trying to run over Kevin. "Would he have any reason to write that message?"

"I can't think of any."

"I've asked Carla this question and now I'm going to ask you. Did you write it to get out of the wedding?"

"My god, no!" Bruce burst out throwing his hands in the air. Those at the nearby tables looked their way. He leaned his arms on the table. "How could you even ask that? I love Carla. I want to marry her."

"Even with the threat hanging over your head?'

"Yes. I'm not going to let some idiot tell me how to live my life."

"You said your father died six years ago and your mother is in a home, so neither of them could be objecting to your wedding. You only have Mason on your father's side, but you never mentioned any on your mother's."

"Because there are none worth mentioning."

"Oh?" Jenna waited for him to continue.

"Okay," he sighed. "My mom was raised in Winnipeg with her three younger sisters. Dad was a drummer in a band that played in bars around the city. Mom was nineteen and worked in an office and one Friday evening she and a couple of her girlfriends went out to a bar. Dad's band was playing there and according to the story he told, it was love at first sight when he saw mom.

"He boldly went up to the table she was at and told her he would really like it if she would wait for him after his gig. In spite of her friends' protests that he was only looking for a one-night stand, she did. They spent the night together at his apartment and the rest is history."

"They married and lived happily ever after," Jenna said.

"Not quite. When her parents found out, they were horrified that their daughter would date a drummer who played in bars and they forbade her from seeing him. She laughed and said she was old enough to date anyone she wanted. So they kicked her out. She moved in with Dad who was actually using the money from playing in bars to put himself through university.

"He graduated and they married at the courthouse without any of her family there. They moved here to Vancouver where I was born. My grandparents are dead on mom's side, but the last I knew my three aunts still live in Winnipeg and I have a total of seven cousins whom I've never met."

"Your mom never saw her parents or sisters again?"

"No. My grandparents were very religious and I guess some pretty strong words were used to describe my father and what she and he were doing together. They never asked for forgiveness and she could not forgive them. As for her sisters, she figured her parents poisoned them against her and Dad, and they never once tried to get in touch with her."

"Wow, that's a lot of years to have animosity against your family. Did you ever try to contact your grandparents or aunts?"

"No. I had Dad's parents with whom I spent a lot of time. As I was growing up, I never really thought about my mom's side of the family because they were never mentioned. I had a life that had never involved them so as an adult I have no reason to find them."

"So we can rule out anyone on your mom's side of the family." Now was the time to get to the point. "And you can't think of anyone from your past who might want to stop the wedding? Some old girlfriend or business associate?"

"You keep asking that question. Why?"

Jenna took a deep breath. "I know about you and Linda."

Bruce sat and stared at Jenna. She felt he was trying to decide if he should admit or deny it.

"Who told you?"

"Mason told Adam."

"That bastard, Mason!"

Heads around them turned in their direction again. He ran his fingers through his hair in exasperation. "I knew as soon as I saw Ronnie had brought Linda as his plus one that someone was going to cause trouble."

Jenna scrutinized the man across from her. He didn't seem at all remorseful about what he'd done, just angry that word had gotten out about it.

"Are you going to tell Carla?" Bruce asked.

"As Carla's friend, I'm disgusted at you for doing that to her and I'm torn about whether I should tell her. I don't want to ruin her happiness, but I also don't like the fact that you cheated on her. And as a dating coach, I would highly recommend to her that she break up with you. Once a cheat, always a cheat."

"But it was all a mistake. It shouldn't have happened."

"Well, it did," Jenna spat out. In spite of herself, she was getting angry with this man. "Tell me how this so-called mistake happened."

"Ronnie invited me out for a few drinks. Linda showed up after about an hour and we started talking about our time together and the fun we had. It was a combination of nostalgia and the booze that made me accept her invitation to go to her place. We only saw each other a few times and then I came to my senses and said it was over."

Jenna had calmed down. "How did she take it? Would she have left you that note?"

"I don't think so," Bruce said. "We both understood it was just a quick hook-up for old times' sake."

It was okay that he understood it that way, but to presume that Linda did also was a big assumption. Maybe Linda hadn't been so understanding. That was another question she had to ask Linda this evening.

"You and Ronnie have been friends for a long time and friends, like spouses, can have bumpy relationships. Other than the motorcycle incident, have you had any more disputes?"

"Of course. But nothing drastic, nothing that would make him want to stop my wedding to Carla."

"Okay. Is there anything else you can add that might help us solve this mystery?" He hadn't mentioned Carla's affair with Rachael. Maybe she hadn't told him yet. Jenna decided it was not her place to tell him, since it happened long before Carla met Bruce. But they each had a secret, and that was not a good start to a marriage.

"No. I've done a lot of thinking about it and there's no one I can think of who would want to harm me."

"Well, if something comes to mind, let me know."

"Have you and Adam been able to learn anything about the note?"

"Unfortunately, nothing concrete so far." Jenna stood. "Thank you for seeing me." She walked away from the table and hurried back to the store. She had a meeting with Ray Weaver, the man with the unusual moving business.

CHAPTER 23

*B*ack at the bookstore, Adam listened as Jenna described her conversation with Bruce, "He did admit to the short affair with Linda. According to him, they both were okay with the breakup. I want to ask Linda how she felt about it tonight."

"Have you decided if you are going to tell Carla?"

"Bruce asked me that and I'm torn. I really hate to cause her more heartbreak than she is going through right now over this whole thing. But I don't like the idea of him sneaking around behind her back, because as far as I am concerned if he did it once, he'll do it again."

"Probably."

"But there is something else. From the way he described meeting up with Linda, it sounds like maybe Ronnie and/or Linda set it all up. Her sudden appearance while they are having a drink in a bar seems a little suspicious. The question is, why would he, or they, do it? There seems to be an underlying conflict between the two best friends that has to do with more than a wrecked motorcycle decades ago."

"Yes," Adam agreed. "It makes you wonder what kind of friend Ronnie is if he would set Bruce up like that after Bruce becomes engaged. Either he doesn't have any loyalty or he has a vicious streak in him and likes to feel the power of holding something over someone."

"So you think he set Bruce up in order to blackmail him?"

"That could be one reason."

"According to Bruce, there have been a few arguments between them but nothing serious," Jenna said. "Would you be able to contact Ronnie for his take on that?"

"I'll send him a text."

"That's my Private Dick," Jenna grinned. "Always willing to take one for the team."

Their conversation ended while they served their customers. When the rush was over, they continued.

"I saw a story last night on one of the true crime shows I watch about a woman named Celeste Beard," Adam said. "She had an affair with another woman named Tracey Tarlton who had some emotional problems. This Celeste convinced Tracey to kill Celeste's wealthy husband so they could be together. It made me wonder if maybe Carla is doing the same with Rachael."

Jenna stared thoughtfully at Adam. "Well, Carla did turn to Rachael after Roger died. But Carla wouldn't get Rachael to threaten Bruce. She would just break up with him."

"We sure have done a lot of speculating with nothing coming of it," Adam said. "The only conflict that we really know about is Monica and Kevin arguing."

"And as far as we know, Kevin didn't even know Carla and Bruce until he started dating Monica."

Adam decided to test the theory he had come up with the night before, "What if we look at Carla's other fiancés' deaths? It just seems like too much of a coincidence that two of the men Carla was engaged to are now dead and the third threatened. We know Dale was murdered in a robbery but what if it was made to look like robbery and Roger was pushed off his balcony?"

"Okay. So then the question would be, by whom?" Jenna said.

This was going to be tricky. "Please let me finish before you say anything." Adam took a deep breath and spoke fast, "Last night, I looked up black widow murderers on the Internet. On one of the websites was a list and write-up of women who'd killed their husbands for their insurance. They dated from the early 1900s to just a few years ago and took place in countries all over the world.

"There was even one here in Canada. The 'black widow' name comes from the black widow spider who eats her mate after sex. The women usually use poison to kill but some have shot their victims. Some have killed more than one husband and sometimes other members of their families."

Adam paused. This was where it got delicate. "What if Carla is a black widow murderer?" He watched for a reaction but Jenna just stared at him with her mouth open.

"I don't know what to say to that," Jenna finally said. "Except Carla didn't inherit any money from Dale or Roger. And with as successful as she is, she doesn't need it."

"What if it isn't the money she's after? What if she likes the romance of being proposed to and agreeing to get married, but doesn't like the idea of actually marrying? What if, rather than break up and look like it's a failed relationship, she kills them to end it and comes off looking like the bereaved fiancée. She would certainly get a lot of sympathy that way."

Jenna started shaking her head.

Adam hastily continued, "In the mid-1960s, there was a woman named Janie Lou Gibbs who murdered her husband with rat poison. She revelled in the expression of sympathy and compassion she received from her family, friends, and her church so much that she decided to kill the rest of her family."

"Do you really think Carla could do such a thing?"

"I don't know but it's something to think about. It would explain the other deaths."

"But why leave Bruce a note?" Jenna asked. "Why try to scare him off?"

"That's the beginning of the plan. It gets the excitement flowing. She wonders if he will leave or stay with her. If he leaves then the game is over. If he stays then she has to find a way to get rid of him."

"But the death of three fiancés would look pretty suspicious."

"Some of the black widows killed multiple times before being arrested. Blanche Moore murdered two husbands, her mother-in-law, her father, and a boyfriend. Nannie Doss killed eleven of her family members. These women somehow got away with it, so maybe Carla thinks she can too."

"No, I don't believe it." Jenna shook her head. "That's not the Carla I know."

"Okay." Adam decided not to push it any more. He'd planted a seed and now would wait to see if it grew. "Then it comes down to who doesn't want Carla to marry?"

"Well, we have Rachael. But she didn't strike me as being easily manipulated so she wouldn't be killing the men at Carla's request or to get her back."

"What about relatives who didn't want the wedding to take place? Carla's mom wasn't there but Monica was."

"What reason would Monica have to want the wedding called off? She made a point of wanting a double wedding."

"Or so she said. That could have been all an act."

"Why, though?"

"No idea."

The bell over the door clanged and a man entered.

"Hello Ray," Jenna said, going around the counter. "Let's go to the café for our practice date."

Adam watched them leave the store. Had Jenna blushed a little when she saw him? Had her voice changed? Was it possible she was attracted to one of her own clients? Adam wondered if there was some sort of rule about a dating coach dating one of her own clients. He hoped not. He hadn't seen her look so pleased to see someone in a long time.

Adam's phone vibrated in his pocket. He pulled it out and saw the name Bill. "About time," he muttered. "Hello."

"Adam, it's Bill. Sorry it's taken me so long to get back to you. My days are long."

"No problem."

"So, what do you want to know? And before you ask, I had nothing to do with the post on my Facebook page and I don't know who hacked it."

"Okay. Did you see anything out of the ordinary at the engagement party, someone sneaking around the head table?"

"I don't remember a lot. It was such a fun party that I didn't pay much attention to the other people around me. I danced, ate, and drank, all the things you're supposed to do at a party."

"Do you have any idea who would have left the piece of paper with the warning on it?"

"None whatsoever."

"So there was no animosity among you men." Adam decided to take a stab in the dark. "Nothing to do with the disappearance of Mason's sister, Destiny."

There was silence on the other end, then finally. "Why do you ask that?"

Adam didn't know for sure. It was just that both Bruce and Ronnie had basically said the same thing about her disappearance having nothing to do with the note. It made him think that it might. But he didn't know in what way.

"Just something Ronnie and Bruce said. I understand you dated her."

"Yes, for a while. So did Ronnie. But he fell in love with her and wanted to marry her. She turned him down and broke up with him."

Oh, this was new. "Was he mad at her?"

"Actually, he was mad at both Destiny and me because I began dating her again."

"Again?"

"Yes. We'd dated before she got together with Ronnie. She came back to me after they split up."

Now, why didn't Ronnie tell me that? Adam wondered. "She was seeing you when she vanished?"

"Yes, but obviously not exclusively, since her girlfriends said she had a date on the day she disappeared. That date wasn't with me. I was at work in my dad's store all day. And yes, the police checked."

"Could the boy she was meeting have been with Ronnie?"

"No, he and Bruce had gone fishing that day. The police also checked their alibis and those of everyone else who knew her. When they couldn't find anyone who may have harmed her, they began to think that she'd simply run away."

"How did you feel about her?"

"I really missed her but not as much as Ronnie. He started drinking and he talked about her and how much he'd loved her when he was drunk. He was smashed most of the summer."

"What do you think happened to her?"

Again, another long pause. "I don't know. But we seem to have gotten off topic. Do you have any more questions about the threat to Bruce?"

"No, but if you do think of something would you let me know?"

"Definitely."

"Thank you." Adam hung up.

Later when Jenna returned from her fake date with Ray he told her what he'd learned.

"Now, we could add an old jealousy to the list of troubles among the three friends," Jenna said.

People began to trickle in for the open mic. Many of them carried an envelope or binder. For the past half hour, Jenna had been pushing aside the shelves on wheels and setting up the wooden podium and chairs for the open mic. The area was small enough that they didn't need a microphone. But not knowing what else to call the gathering they stuck with the open mic name. Most of the attendees spaced themselves out in the chairs in the last row. Jenna wondered if one of the women was Linda. She decided she would have to wait for Linda to stand for her reading.

"How many do you think will be attending?" Jenna asked Adam as they stood by the counter. There'd been a lot of inquiries over the last few days but that seldom translated into people showing up.

"We know at least eight, because that's how many have signed up to do a reading."

"And sometimes, that's all we get," Jenna laughed. Not that she minded. That usually meant there was more discussion afterwards. It gave the first-time readers a chance to get to know other writers in the area.

Adam's phone vibrated in his pocket. He read the text message. "Ronnie can meet me tomorrow evening after work," he told Jenna.

"Good." Jenna was putting the snacks on the small table in the corner. "Maybe we can learn something more about his and Bruce's strange relationship."

Adam went to the front. "If you are interested in the two-minute, speed reading segment of tonight's entertainment, you can sign up on the sheet of paper on that shelf." He pointed to the shelving holding the cookbook section.

"Hi, Jenna."

Jenna turned and smiled. "So nice that you made it, Sophia."

"I'm a little scared," Sophia whispered. "I've never read my work-in-progress to an audience before. It's always after it's been published."

"You'll be fine," Jenna said. "We're all friendly here. Did your sister come as well?"

"No. Edna has a headache."

"Oh, that's too bad."

"I think it's just a ruse to get out of speaking to a bunch of people. She's never felt comfortable doing it."

"Well, find yourself a chair and get ready to have some fun."

Eventually, most of the chairs were filled and there was a smattering of talk as some saw others they knew. At five-thirty, Jenna went to the podium and cleared her throat.

"Good evening and welcome to our monthly open mic. We're glad you could come and either do a reading or listen to our talented Vancouver writers. Our first reader is Bethany."

There was a smattering of applause and a teen aged girl stood and carried a binder to the front. She set it on the podium.

"Tonight, I'd like to read the short story I've written titled, *Among You and Me*." Bethany's voice was strong and clear. The story wasn't long and she finished to a round of loud applause.

"Next up is Paul."

Paul read from a manuscript he was working on and after him, Stephen read a poem. Jenna introduced Sophia who gave a little speech about how she and her sister had switched from writing true crime novels to fiction mysteries.

"We found ourselves getting too old to chase down all the leads and to speak with everyone involved in solving a real murder so we decided to write a fiction novel." She held up some papers. "This is a few pages of our first chapter where we are setting up the plot and the characters involved." She began reading.

Linda turned out to be the tall, slender blonde who had come in just before Jenna started the evening. She'd slid into an empty chair at the end of the second last row. Now that her name was called, she appeared hesitant. Jenna thought she might back out and smiled encouragingly at her. Finally she stood and walked to the front.

"I've just begun writing poetry and I don't know if it is any good. Of course, my family praises my efforts but I'm hoping I can get some feedback tonight from any of you who wish to comment." Linda launched into her poem about lost love and betrayal.

Jenna wondered if the occurrence described in the poem was from Linda's own experience, like her love affair with Bruce. If it was, she'd taken the break-up hard, harder than Bruce had said. Jenna made a note to ask her.

Adam walked up to the podium when the last of the regular readers had finished and called the first of the two-minute speed readers. There were five.

"Well, that was one of the best evenings we've had for a long time," Adam said at the end. "Thank you everyone for coming. Please stay and enjoy a snack while talking with a writer whose story or poem you liked. When you wish to leave, let Jenna or myself know and we'll escort you to the outside door." It was up to them to make sure everyone left the building so while one stayed in the store, the other showed the people out.

There was scuffling and scraping as people stood and stretched and pushed their chairs aside. Some headed to the table, while others began to talk immediately. Jenna saw that Linda was standing by herself. She was just about to head over to her when Adam appeared at her side. He said something and Linda smiled up at him. Jenna decided to leave them alone. He was probably complimenting her on her poetry which she herself had found very moving.

CHAPTER 24

"So, tell us about you and Bruce," Adam said. He and Jenna had put the chairs away and returned the bookshelves to their rightful places and then walked with Linda to The Keg. They'd ordered drinks and some appetizers.

"Not much to tell. He was a friend of my cousin and I saw him a few times at parties as we were growing up. I moved away for university and then returned after graduation and took a job here. We met up again when we were in our thirties and started going out. We lived together for five years before splitting up."

"So, you're the five-year relationship Bruce told me about," Jenna said. "Why did you break up?"

"We weren't going anywhere. Neither of us wanted to get married at the time and we just drifted apart."

"But you two hooked up again just a while ago, after Bruce got engaged to Carla. Why?"

Linda blushed and looked down at her hands. "That was a mistake."

The server came over with their drinks, three small plates, and cutlery.

"Did you and Ronnie set up the meeting with Bruce that night in the bar?" Adam asked—might as well get to the point.

Linda gasped and looked at him, "No! I would never do that!"

"How did you happen to show up where he and Bruce were having a drink?" Jenna asked.

"Ronnie invited me to the bar. We'd been talking about putting on a surprise party for my brother's fortieth birthday and he said he had some great ideas."

"What did you do when you saw Bruce was with him?" Jenna took a sip of her drink.

"I never thought anything of it. They're friends."

"And you all got drunk."

"Pretty much. Ronnie kept ordering drinks and Bruce and I were having fun reminiscing about the holidays we'd taken, the downhill skiing we'd done, the parties we'd put on while we'd lived together."

The server set two plates, one of mushroom caps stuffed with crab and cream cheese and one of lightly fried calamari, on the table.

"Whose idea was it to go back to your place?" Adam scooped some calamari and two mushroom caps onto his plate. He was hungry, only being able to grab a quick salad at lunch.

"I think Ronnie came up with it." Linda took a mushroom cap and a couple of calamari. "He said we belonged together and we should give ourselves another chance. I was drunk enough to ask Bruce and he was drunk enough to accept."

"Did you know that he was engaged to Carla?"

"No. Honestly, I hadn't heard that."

"How did you feel when Bruce decided to break it off?"

"Did he tell you that?" Linda shook her head. "I can't believe he's still lying. He didn't break it off. I did as soon as I heard about his engagement."

Adam looked at Jenna and raised an eyebrow. She shrugged her shoulders. This was another lie in a string of lies they'd uncovered.

"I'd suspected he was having affairs while we were together," Linda continued. "I guess that was confirmed when he slept with me while planning his wedding to Carla."

218

Adam chewed on a mushroom cap trying to think of something else to ask. "Why would Ronnie invite you to the engagement party?"

"There is something funny about his and Bruce's friendship, almost like they are being held together because of a shared secret or something."

"What do you mean?"

"Ronnie sometimes seems scared of Bruce. He pushes Bruce, doing things like parading me at his engagement party, but only to a certain point and then he backs off. Almost like Bruce has something over him and Ronnie hates it and tries to get back at him in petty little ways."

"And you have no idea what it is?"

"No, but they've been competitive since they were kids. One always had to prove he was better at swimming, or baseball, or getting girls. In adulthood, they had to see who had the best physique, who was better at playing the stock market, and who had the most conquests. Maybe one of their competitions went wrong somehow."

"Why did you go to the party?" Jenna asked.

Linda smiled slightly. "It was my way of getting back at Bruce for the times he was unfaithful while we were together. I just wanted to see him squirm a little. I didn't talk with him but I went up to Carla and spoke to her while he was watching."

"It looks like Ronnie may have set you both up," Jenna said. "Has he tried to blackmail you about your short affair with Bruce?"

"No," Linda snorted. "I haven't had a steady relationship with anyone for over a year. There's no one who would be mad at me."

"I'm a dating coach, if you ever want to try finding the right man." Jenna took a card from her purse and handed it to Linda. "I've had a lot of success setting people up together."

"Yes, she has," Adam said. "She has even been invited to a wedding."

"Thank you." Linda put the card in her pocket.

"Do you think Ronnie could be blackmailing Bruce?" Adam asked. "Using your affair to get him to do something?"

"I wouldn't put it past him," Linda said. "That could be why he did it. But I can't think what he would want from Bruce. They're already going into business together, something Ronnie told me recently he'd wanted to do for years. And that was a bit of a shock since he'd always said he liked the freedom of working for someone else.

"That way he didn't have to worry about making a profit or put up with employees not showing up for work, none of the headaches of owning his own business. He liked that his day ended at five o'clock and his weekends were free." She glanced at her watch. "Do you have any more questions? I have to get going."

Adam shook his head. "I think that's all." He looked at Jenna.

"I have no more," Jenna said. "Thank you for coming."

"If it will stop another woman from being screwed by Bruce, then I'll do anything." Linda stood and left the restaurant.

Adam looked at the time on his cell phone. "It's nine o'clock. Should we go see Kevin?"

"Sounds good to me."

After Adam paid for the drinks and snacks, they headed to Jenna's car.

"Well, we learned a little more, but still not enough to figure out who left the note."

"Maybe we're not asking the right questions," Jenna said, as they drove to the hospital.

"I thought we were asking great questions, getting right to the point, finding out people's history together. I don't know what else we could be doing."

Jenna found a parking spot and they walked a block to the hospital. As they waited for the elevator, they looked around hoping that they wouldn't run in to Monica. They rode up to the men's ward and Adam asked for Kevin Barkley's room at the nursing station.

"Last room on the right down that hall."

Jenna led the way. Adam saw there were two names on the wall beside the door. They would have to be careful about the questions they asked. Kevin was in his bed watching a small television. His head was bandaged and his right wrist was in a cast. A curtain was drawn between the two beds. Neither man had visitors.

"Hi, Kevin," Jenna smiled, going up to his bed.

He looked up at her without recognition.

"I'm Monica's friend. We met at the Alliance Theatre last week."

"Oh, yeah." He turned the sound down on the television.

"This is my business partner, Adam," Jenna introduced.

Adam didn't think Kevin would want to shake hands so he waved. "Hello."

"Monica and Carla stopped by our bookstore this morning and told us about someone trying to run you down," Jenna said. "We're glad that you weren't hurt very bad."

"It would have been better if I hadn't been hurt at all," Kevin said.

"Do you know who did it?" Adam asked, getting to the point of their visit. Monica or someone else might show up at any time.

"No."

"I know I already asked you about the piece of paper left on the head table but I'm wondering if there is something you might be able to tell us that you couldn't say in front of Monica."

"I know nothing about it. Why would I? I barely know them."

One of the things Adam had learned from watching the true crime shows is that if someone answers a question by asking another question, they might have something to hide.

"What are you two doing here?" a voice demanded.

Adam and Jenna turned to see Monica striding towards them.

"We just wanted to see how he was doing," Jenna said.

"No, you wanted to ask him questions about us after I specifically told you to leave him alone."

A nurse hurried into the room. "Please keep your voices down," she said. "We have patients sleeping."

"Sorry," Jenna apologized. "We're just leaving."

Adam followed Jenna out the door and down the hall. "She really doesn't want us to talk to him," Adam said, as they waited for the elevators.

"And I wonder why. What does he know that she doesn't want us to find out?"

"That's the big question and another one is, does it have anything to do with Bruce and Carla or is there something in her and Kevin's relationship that she's hiding?"

"Well, I'll drive you home and we can sleep on it. Maybe we have to let our subconscious stew over it for a while."

"I hope something stews on it," Adam grinned. "Because I'm all out of ideas." His phone pinged and he looked at the message. He raised his eyebrows.

"What?' Jenna asked.

"Mason is at the Numbers Cabaret and he's invited me for a late drink."

"That sounds promising. I'll drop you off."

"Okay." Adam sent a message back to Mason.

CHAPTER 25

"So, how was your drink with Mason last night?" Jenna asked Adam Sunday morning. Michele hadn't been able to work, so both of them had opened the store.

"Well, we cleared up a few things," Adam said. "He admitted he likes to flirt but he remains true when he's in a permanent relationship."

"Good," Jenna nodded.

"Also, he's a closet romance writer."

"A what?"

"He writes LGBTQ romance novels under a pseudonym and that's how he supplements his income. He hopes to eventually become a full-time writer and quit being a flight attendant."

"Maybe we can have him in for a reading and signing sometime," Jenna said.

Adam smiled. "I already mentioned that to him and he said he'd think about it. And as for his credit card, he'd forgotten that it had expired and he'd received a new one. It took him a while to find the envelope in his stack of old mail."

"I've thought about what you said yesterday about Carla killing her fiancés to get out of marrying them," Jenna said, changing subjects. "I don't believe it. I've known her through all her engagements and her grief was genuine each time. I think she truly wants to get married."

"Okay," Adam said. "What about doing it for all the attention and caring and concern from others?"

"No. She doesn't like to bring attention to herself. I've seen her accidently cut herself and try to hide it. She is almost shy that way."

"Could Carla and Bruce be in this together?"

"To what end?"

"No idea. Just something my subconscious spit out from stewing all night," Adam grinned.

Jenna smiled in return. Her phone rang and she picked it up. "Morning Carla."

"Jenna, I just heard about your visit to see Kevin. Monica isn't happy about it."

"Why isn't she?" Jenna asked. She walked away from the counter as a customer came up to pay for a book. "What is she trying to hide?"

"She isn't trying to hide anything. She just doesn't want you harassing Kevin about something that has nothing to do with him. Please don't try to speak with him again."

"All right," Jenna said, reluctantly. "If you're sure."

"I'm sure. And nothing more has occurred in the past week. Maybe I overreacted to the note because of my past history."

"I don't think you overreacted. It was a normal response to a scary situation. I'm sorry that Adam and I haven't had any success at finding out who could have left it and why. We've considered that it could be a bad joke someone was playing." It might be time to admit defeat.

"Well, it wasn't very funny. Thank you for all the work you've done. You could be right about someone having a sick sense of humour. Maybe I can quit this constant worrying. It gets tiring after a while."

Jenna hung up and walked back to Adam. "It seems Monica wants us called off Kevin."

"Really?"

"Yes. So, I said that since we don't seem to be any closer to finding out anything about the note than we were a week ago, that maybe we should accept that it was a joke."

"What did Carla say to that?"

"She seemed unwilling at first but finally agreed."

"So our sleuthing days are over. We are back to being mere store owners."

"As much as I hate to admit it, it appears that way." Jenna looked around the store. Only one customer. "It's back to normal life. I'm going to the office to write my next dating coach blog. Call me if it gets busy."

In the office, Jenna opened her computer to Word and stared at the screen. She just didn't feel right about dropping the search for whoever was behind the threat to Bruce. There were some things that still bothered her, too many unanswered questions. After a few minutes of thought, she went back to the front.

Adam grinned. "Can't leave it alone, either?"

"No. There are just too many things that don't add up."

"I agree. Shall we go over them?"

"Okay. Bruce and Ronnie have been friends since childhood but they don't seem to like each other much. Ronnie basically set Bruce up with Linda and then rubbed his nose in his affair by taking Linda to the engagement party."

"Bruce claims to love Carla but had no hesitation or even regret about fooling around on her," Adam said.

"I feel like a traitor by keeping my mouth shut about that. Maybe he'll step up and admit it now that more people know."

"That will be hard on her if he does."

"And harder if he doesn't and they get married," Jenna said. "She'll eventually find out."

"To continue, Monica and Kevin are engaged but there is something weird about it. They hadn't been dating long before Kevin proposed, they seem to fight a lot, Kevin was seen kissing another woman, and someone tried to run him down."

"Was it accidental or intentional? If intentional, who was driving and were they trying to scare him or kill him? And was it related to the car that tried to hit us?"

"And to bring up one of my theories," Adam said. "Rachael still cares for Carla. Is she trying to get rid of Bruce?"

"But what would she have against Kevin?"

"Don't know. Do you think his attempted run-over is associated with the note? Could they be two separate incidents?"

Jenna shook her head. "My god, too many questions and not enough answers."

"On the bright side, it looks like we can rule out Lillian and Bill."

"Well, it was Bill who posted on Facebook about the note."

"He said he'd been hacked and changed his page," Adam said. "Nothing more has appeared since. And there was the odd way that both Bruce and Ronnie said about Destiny's death having nothing to do with this. And I just remembered that Ronnie said Destiny may have been abducted and murdered just like Bruce did. Granted, those were the words used in the news articles I read."

Adam grimaced. "Sounds like I'm arguing against myself."

"There was something Monica said yesterday when she and Carla came to tell us about Kevin that bothered me but I can't figure out what it was."

"Well, let's go over it." Adam waved to the door. "They rushed in here to tell us Kevin was in the hospital because he'd been hit by a car. Monica had found him on her way to her car."

"That's it!" Jenna squealed. "She said she found him on her way to her car but when Carla and I went to see her after opening night of the play, she told us she parks on the street because it was safer when she works late."

"So why was she going to her car in the lot?"

"Right. Why?"

"She could have parked it there that night for some good reason," Adam pointed out.

"Awfully strange that she would on the one night that someone tries to run over Kevin. He was leaving before her because he was getting up early the next morning. What if, instead of changing and removing her make-up, she hurried out the front of the theatre to her car, drove around to the lot, and waited for Kevin to come out of the building? When she saw him she tried to hit him."

"Then afterwards, she parked her car and went back inside to change. When no one else found Kevin, she had to go out and do it herself and told the police she was on her way to her car. I wonder if the police actually checked to make sure her car was in the lot like she claimed."

"That would have been the chance she had to take. She couldn't park it there just in case Kevin was conscious and saw or heard her do it."

"So what do we do about this? Phone her and ask?"

"That's one option but, I doubt she'll talk with us."

"Unless you apologize for visiting Kevin," Adam grinned wickedly. "You were just concerned since he's engaged to your friend's sister and that sister is a woman whom you like and admire."

"That's laying it on a bit thick, don't you think?" Jenna laughed.

"I'll serve this young lady while you decide." Adam smiled at a teen who was holding three books and a mug with the saying 'All my weekends are booked'. "Cute mug isn't it?"

"Yes," she said. "It's for my mother's birthday. She loves to read."

Jenna dialed a number as she walked away from the counter.

"What do you want?" Monica asked.

"First of all, I want to apologize for last night. Adam and I were concerned about Kevin since he is going to be my friend's brother-in-law." Jenna grimaced as she said that. It sounded so lame.

"Okay, apology accepted. Anything else?"

"Just one thing. You told me you park on the street when at the theatre at night for safety purposes. Yet you told us yesterday you were on your way to your car in the parking lot when you found Kevin."

"Really? You're accusing me of trying to run over Kevin?"

"No, just wondering why you parked in the lot that night?"

"That's none of your business." Monica disconnected.

Jenna stared at her phone wondering if she should talk with Carla about the discrepancy. She decided not to. Carla hadn't been very happy that she was bothering Monica. No use upsetting her more.

"Well, buttering up Monica didn't work," Jenna told Adam, as she walked behind the counter.

"You called her?"

"Yes, and she told me where she parked was none of my business."

"So, where does that leave us?"

"It leaves me writing my blog and you serving customers," Jenna said. She walked back to the office and once again brought up Word. She stared at the blank page, willing an idea for her blog to appear. But a little voice in her head kept asking the same questions she and Adam had been posing for the last week.

What if someone had a grudge against Bruce and used Carla's past as a diversion to get to him?

Who didn't want either Carla or Bruce to marry?

Why would Ronnie set Bruce up with Linda? What would he gain?

Why would Monica want to get engaged to someone whom she didn't seem to love? Why would Kevin want to get engaged to her?

Jenna let her mind go back over the past week and all the conversations she and Adam had had with the members of the head table and she started to see a pattern. Could that really be the way it was?

Jenna's phone rang. She saw Carla's name and number on the screen. Did she want to talk with her now or wait until she had digested her theory? She decided to answer it.

"Hi, Carla."

"Monica called and told me you phoned her and basically accused her of trying to kill Kevin. What's wrong with you? Why are you making such absurd accusations?"

"Can Adam and I meet with you and Bruce this evening?" Jenna asked.

"What for?"

"I think I may have come up with who left the note and why."

"Well, don't wait until tonight. Tell me now."

Jenna could hear the impatience in Carla's voice but she didn't want to say anything over the phone nor did she want to tell just Carla. Bruce needed to be there, too. "It would be best if it was the two of you and even Monica and Ronnie if you could invite them."

"Okay, if you insist," Carla said.

"We'll be at your place around six-thirty." Jenna said, quietly.

Carla hung up without a goodbye.

Jenna went to the front. There was a line-up at the counter.

"Finished already?" Adam asked, as he bagged two books for a customer.

"Haven't started." Jenna went to the other cash register. "I'll take the next person in line," she said.

It was an hour before Jenna could run her theory past Adam. He looked shocked and then slowly nodded. "That does answer all our questions," he said.

"That's what I thought. I told Carla we'd be there after we close the store to tell her and Bruce. I also asked her to invite Monica and Ronnie."

CHAPTER 26

Jenna and Adam left the Net Loft and headed to Jenna's parking spot. It was getting darker earlier each day and the streetlights were on casting a dim light on the pavement. In spite of it being near the end of October, the evening was warm and there were few vehicles.

Jenna was able to find a parking spot close to Carla's condo and they walked into the entrance. Jenna took a deep breath before pushing Carla's buzzer.

"This is going to be hard on a lot of people if you are right," Adam said.

"I know," Jenna said, as the lock clicked and she opened the door. "In a way, I'm hoping I'm wrong. Either way, it may affect Carla's and my friendship. You know that saying about not shooting the messenger."

They rode the elevator to Carla's floor and knocked on her door. She opened it and ushered them in. Bruce was sitting on the couch.

"Monica will be here shortly and Ronnie said he had previous plans," Carla said, as she motioned for them to sit.

"What's this about?" Bruce asked. "You've upset Carla so it had better be good."

The atmosphere in the room was cool. Jenna decided to get right to one of the reasons for their visit. No use exchanging pleasantries. She looked at Bruce.

"Ronnie killed Destiny, didn't he?" Jenna heard Carla gasp but didn't look at her.

"What?" Bruce asked, a shocked and fearful look on his face. He recovered quickly. "No. Where did you get that stupid idea from?"

Jenna knew by his initial reaction the accusation was true. She had guessed right and she ignored his denial.

"Was it the time he stole your motorcycle or one of the times he borrowed your car?" she asked.

"Is it true?" Carla stared open-mouthed at Bruce. "Did he kill her?"

"Did you help him get rid of the body?" Jenna continued when he didn't answer Carla's question. "Have you been blackmailing him ever since?"

"Stop it!" Carla jumped up and yelled at Jenna. "Stop saying those things." She turned and looked down at Bruce. "Say something. Tell her she's wrong."

Bruce stood. "I don't have to stay here and take this. I'm leaving."

"The police are on their way," Adam said. "We've already told them everything. You won't get far."

Bruce stared at Adam as if trying to decide if he should run then he dropped back onto the couch. He buried his head in his hands. "How did you find out?" he asked, in an anguished voice.

"Just pieced together bits of different conversations," Jenna said. "Ronnie told Adam he had dated Destiny when they were teenagers. He made it sound like it was only a few times but Bill said Ronnie loved Destiny and wanted to marry her but she broke up with him and went back to Bill.

"Everyone said the night she disappeared she was supposed to be meeting a boy. Bill said it wasn't him. You told us Ronnie only borrowed your car to take the girl he loved up to Cypress

Mountain Provincial Park. Bill said Ronnie loved Destiny and wanted to marry her."

"Ronnie and I were fishing the day she disappeared." He looked up. "We had nothing to do with it."

"How convenient that you were each other's alibi," Jenna said, dryly. She continued with her questioning, "Did Ronnie take her to the park and, when she spurned his love, did he kill her?"

Bruce didn't answer.

"Do you want to tell us how it happened?" Adam asked.

"I guess it's time to end this." Bruce took a deep breath. "Ronnie really loved Destiny and he wanted to get her back. He borrowed my car and got her to agree to meet him at Park Royal and go for a drive with him. He proposed to her for the second time and she turned him down again. He told me he wanted to prove his love for her but she clawed and kicked at him and started screaming.

"He lost control and hit her a few times to stop her but she wouldn't quit so he put his hands around her throat to shut her up. When he finally regained his senses he realized he'd choked her to death. He was so scared that he drove her body to my house."

"And you helped him hide her?"

"Yes."

"How could you, Bruce?" Carla gasped. "She was your cousin, Mason's sister."

"He was in shock and he kept begging me to do something. I... I didn't know what else to do. We were just kids and he was my best friend."

"So, his friendship was more important than her being your cousin," Jenna said.

"Yes. No." Bruce rubbed his hands over his face. "I didn't know what else to do," he repeated.

"And you thought the knowledge would be useful in the future," Adam said. "Was his family rich?"

Bruce sighed, "Not really. But his grandmother had left him a trust fund which he didn't have access to until he reached twenty-one."

"So you bided your time and tapped into his money whenever you wanted to."

Bruce never answered.

Carla's phone buzzed and she pushed a number. "Monica is here."

Bruce was just the warmup act, Jenna thought. *Now for the main attraction.* She looked at Adam for support and he gave a half smile and a nod. She nodded back.

The door opened and Monica walked in. She saw the small group and, as if sensing the tension in the air, stopped and looked from Carla to Jenna.

"We've just had a bit of bad news," Jenna said.

"What? Did someone die?" Her eyes widened and she gaped at Carla. "Is Mom okay? Did something happen to her?"

"She's fine," Jenna said, when Carla didn't answer. She could see Adam moving to put himself between Monica and the door. "Would you like to sit down?"

Monica eyes flitted from Jenna to Carla then to Bruce who was sitting with his head in his hands again. Jenna couldn't tell if he was crying or not.

"What's going on?" She warily moved farther into the living room.

"Did you want to kill Kevin or just scare him?" Jenna asked.

"Oh, no," Carla moaned. She slumped into one of the overstuffed chairs.

"What are you talking about?" Monica demanded.

"Didn't his acting as your fiancé live up to your standards? Did he keep arguing with you and wanting to see his girlfriend?"

Monica stood with her mouth open. Finally, she gathered her wits. "I don't know where you got such a stupid idea."

Almost the same wording as Bruce. "You'll find out," Jenna said. She hesitated. This was going to be the tough part, not only for her but for Carla. She turned to her friend on the couch.

"I know now that I should have asked this at the very beginning but it didn't seem necessary. Bruce was the one being threatened, not you." She took a deep breath. "Carla, who inherits in your will?"

"What?" Carla seemed confused at the change in direction of the conversation.

"If something happens to you, who are your beneficiaries?"

"Uh, some goes to my mother, but most of my money and assets go to Monica. Why?"

"Because that's the reason you have lost two fiancés and Bruce was threatened."

"I don't understand," Carla said, faintly.

"You will." Jenna turned back to Monica. "Bruce told you he was going to ask Carla to marry him. You'd been worried about that ever since they met because Carla seemed so happy. You had to come up with a plan to try and stop it. First, you threatened or bribed or blackmailed Kevin to pretend to be your fiancé so you could act so pleased with their engagement that you wanted a double wedding."

236

"I don't know what you're talking about. I'm leaving." Monica headed towards the door.

Adam stepped in her way.

"Hey, what's going on? Am I a prisoner here?"

"You will be once the police come," Jenna said. "Now tell us about the note."

"I've told you before that I had nothing to do with it. You all know Kevin and I wanted a double wedding with Carla and Bruce."

"You didn't want a wedding at all, not for you and not for Carla. That's why you killed Dale and Roger."

"That's not true!" Carla cried. She leaped up and put her arm around her sister. "Tell her, Monica! Tell her it isn't true!"

Monica glared at Jenna and for a moment Jenna wondered if she was going to attack her.

"I should have killed you with my car instead of trying to scare you," Monica spat out.

Another mystery solved, Jenna thought. The speeding vehicle that had nearly hit her and Adam had been deliberate. Jenna kept eye contact with Monica and then, just like the inflatable advertising man deflates when the air is let out, Monica sighed and collapsed into a chair. She closed her eyes and laid her head back.

"Did you send them a note like you did Bruce?" Jenna asked.

Monica was silent.

"Did they ignore your threats?"

"I gave them both a chance to back out of the wedding," Monica said, quietly. "I did warn them, but neither of them listened. I disguised my voice and called each of them from a burner phone. Dale actually laughed at me. He thought it was someone playing a joke on him."

She sat up and looked at Jenna. "So, one night when I knew he was working late, I went up to him while he was on his way to the parking lot where he kept his car. It was dark and no one else was around. I asked him if he was sure he really wanted to marry Carla. I pointed out her faults but he was adamant. Then he had the audacity to laugh at me and tell me that he was going to inherit her millions as her husband instead of me."

Carla stared at her sister. "What?"

"Oh yes," Monica smiled. "He was just after your money."

"I don't believe it. He was so attentive, so loving."

"And it worked, didn't it," Monica said. "He got you to agree to marry him. You're lucky I killed him."

"How did you kill him?" Jenna asked.

"I originally went to try and convince him to break off their engagement but I was so angry at what he had said that I shot him."

"You'd taken a gun with you?" Adam asked. "Where did you get it? How did you get it?"

"I bought it from someone on the street. I took it with me to threaten him in case he refused. After I shot him, I reached in his pocket and pulled out his wallet. I was going to take the wallet with me but I decided to leave it so the police had an identity. Plus, I didn't want to get caught with it on me. Money is harder to trace so I just grabbed the bills from it. I was wearing gloves and I took them and the gun and threw them off the Granville Street Bridge."

"How could you?" Carla moaned. "You could have come to me with what he'd said."

"Would you have believed me enough to give him back his ring?"

Carla opened then closed her mouth. "I really did love him."

"Right," Monica nodded. "You would have married him and eventually lost your money to him."

"What about Roger?" Jenna asked.

"Oh, he was easy. He hung up on my phone calls so I kept tabs on what he was doing. Carla, you were the one who told me he was going out to celebrate your engagement with some friends. I went to the same bar at about eleven o'clock and found a table in a dim corner where I could watch while they partied. He was having such a good time that he didn't even notice me.

"They were pretty tipsy when I got there and they kept drinking until midnight when they decided to leave. They all staggered and swayed their way out onto the sidewalk in front of the bar. One of them had driven over and thought he could take them all home while the others wanted to call cabs. They were so drunk they didn't question why I was there when I went up to them. I said I was a friend of Roger's and offered to get him home safely. I think they were happy to leave him with me.

"I got him in my car and drove to his apartment building. I figured there were cameras, so I made sure they could see me struggling to get him into the building and up to his apartment. I dumped him on his couch and took his keys. I left, again knowing any cameras would record me leaving. At about three in the morning, I snuck back and used his keys to get in the rear door. I didn't see any cameras in the stairwell, so I climbed the stairs and let myself into his apartment. It took a while to find his cell phone and I dialed your number, Carla. I know you leave your cell phone in the living room at night so that any calls don't wake you. I just let it ring a couple of times and hung up. It was an effort but I got him up off the couch and out onto the deck. Luckily, he wasn't that big of a man. I heaved him over and threw his cell phone after him."

"Oh, my god." Carla clamped her hands over her mouth. "I can't believe any of this."

"Why did you make the phone call from his cell?" Jenna asked.

"To show the police he was up and on the phone at that time. It would be long after it looked like I'd left, so it would have no connection with me. As it was, the police ruled it an accident and didn't even check the camera footage."

"And why a note this time?"

"There was no suspicion on me after the other two. I'd gotten away with two murders. If a third fiancé died, then the police might look at the other two differently. I thought it best to try a new tactic. I thought with you having two dead fiancés, a threatening note might scare Bruce away. I figured he would take it seriously and have a legitimate reason for calling off the wedding."

"But he didn't."

"No."

Now came the big question. "If you wanted Carla's money so much, why didn't you kill her?"

"What?" Monica looked shocked. "She's my sister. I couldn't kill her."

"So you were willing to wait for her to die from an accident or disease?

Monica seemed surprised at the question. "Yes."

Carla's phone buzzed. She ignored it.

Jenna picked it up. "Someone is downstairs."

240

"That will be the police," Adam said, quietly. He stayed by the door after Jenna buzzed them in and he opened it when they knocked.

Jenna took the lead in explaining about Destiny's murder twenty-five years ago and Bruce's part in hiding her body. Then she told them how Monica was responsible for the deaths of Carla's two fiancés.

"You have been busy," one of the detectives said to Jenna and Adam, as they led Bruce and Monica away.

"It took a while to sort everything out," Jenna said.

"All three of you will have to come down to the station tomorrow to sign formal statements."

"We'll be there."

Jenna and Adam sat in the chairs and watched Carla, who now seemed to be in a dazed trance. They didn't want to leave her alone.

"It's a little saddening to know your sister wished you would die so she could inherit your money," Carla murmured.

"But she didn't want you to die enough to kill you," Jenna pointed out.

"Not much of a comfort," Carla smiled wanly. "Two men died because of that."

CHAPTER 27

"Wow, solving three murders at once," Hillary said. "That must be some sort of record. You two are certainly bang-up 'decrypters.'"

"Well, I wouldn't go that far," Jenna laughed.

It was a week after the encounter with Bruce and Monica and she and Adam were seated with Hillary and Drake at the Sandbar Seafood Restaurant on Granville Island.

"Actually, that would be four if you count Jonathon's hit-and-run killer," Hillary said.

"We didn't have anything to do with that," Jenna said. "That was all Drake."

"I couldn't have done it without your support." Drake raised his glass of beer. "Thank you. It's a real load off my shoulders."

Jenna smiled happily at Drake and clinked glasses with him and the others. Trevor Mayler had been tracked down by the police. He was now a twenty-seven-year-old father of two who worked with families as a children's disabilities services caseworker. He'd been fourteen when he and his friend took his father's car for a joyride and hit Jonathon. His father was prominent in politics and looked after the situation. He sold the car to a friend who stripped it down for parts. He offered to pay for all of Trevor's friend's education and bought him a car to keep him quiet. And he shipped Trevor off to a boarding school in England.

When Trevor returned, he went to university to train as a social worker. Unfortunately, for him, Sean had overdosed and been saved by Drake in the emergency room. Gavin was friends with Trevor's older brother and to repay Drake, Gavin had decided to give him the information about Trevor. When Trevor's father found out about it, he had Gavin killed to save his son and the family name. Sean and his mother coming forward had finally given the police what they needed to solve the mystery.

"What made you clue in about Monica being a killer?" Hillary asked.

"Adam and I went back over all the conversations and realized that it was Monica who kept pointing us in different directions. She suggested to Carla that Roberta and Conrad might be behind the note. She sent the blurry picture of a woman at the head table, a picture she admits she took herself. She told me about Rachael loving Carla. She suggested that Kevin almost getting run over was connected to the note making us wonder if the note was a decoy to get everyone's thinking going in Bruce's direction."

"She got Kevin to hack into Bill's Facebook page and post that message and picture of Carla and Bruce," Adam said. "She hoped there would be an outcry by family and friends over the note and Bruce would call everything off."

"It might have worked, if Carla and Bruce hadn't taken the posts off their sites before anyone saw it," Jenna said.

"Monica was mad at Carla for going to Jenna for dating advice last spring," Adam added. "Then she was even madder when Carla asked us to help her find out who'd left the note. She thought the threat would scare Bruce and it would all be over."

"So Monica wanted her sister's money but she didn't want to murder Carla to get it?"

"Apparently so." Jenna nodded

"But what if Carla lived to be in her eighties or nineties?"

"Monica had it all worked out. She was prepared to wait. Carla had already promised to back her desire to form a production company so if Carla died when Monica was still young enough, she was going to buy a penthouse with a view of the water and mountains. She'd hire cleaning staff and a cook so she didn't have to do any housework. She would travel and buy a condo in Mexico for the winters. If she needed to, she would hire a companion to travel with her and do her bidding. If she was older when Carla died, then she would move into a large one- or two-bedroom suite in the most expensive seniors' home where they have all the amenities like fancy food, laundry services, cleaning staff, parties, entertainment, and all sorts of activities for her to while away her days."

"Monica was willing to wait for Carla to die to inherit, she just didn't want her to marry and that way potentially lose the money to a husband," Adam said.

"What if Monica died first?" Drake asked.

"Then what happened to Carla's money really wouldn't matter to her." Jenna shrugged. "Some people's thinking can't be explained."

"Didn't you say there was a lot of blackmailing and bribery going on also?" Hillary asked.

"Was there ever," Jenna laughed. "Ronnie inherited some money from his grandmother and Bruce blackmailed him into giving him money every time he wanted to buy a brewery franchise. Ronnie had finally demanded to be a partner in the one in Whistler. And Ronnie was in the process of blackmailing Bruce about his affair with his ex-girlfriend to try and get some of his money back."

"Sounds kind of convoluted," Drake said. "And really, neither of them could go to the police without implicating themselves."

"True."

"What about the bribery?" Hillary asked.

"Kevin wanted to get into television and movies," Jenna said. "When Monica found out Bruce was going to propose to Jenna, she told Kevin she knew an agent who was looking for new talent and she would introduce him to the agent if Kevin would pretend to be her fiancé for a couple of months."

"She sure was busy with all her scheming," Hillary said. "So, what's happening with Bruce?"

"The police have charged him with accessory to the murder of his cousin Destiny, committing an indignity to a dead body, and many other offences. Ronnie was charged with Destiny's murder."

Drake looked at Adam. "And she was the sister of your friend, Mason, right?"

"Yes. The police recovered her remains from where Ronnie and Bruce buried her and Mason and his family are finally able to plan her funeral." Adam looked at his watch. "I have to go meet Mason. We're going shopping for a suit for the funeral."

"Say hi to him for me," Jenna said.

"I can't believe that so much has happened since the note was found," Hillary said, watching Adam leave. "It certainly has shaken up a lot of lives. But it looks like one good thing came of it."

"Yes," Jenna agreed. "I haven't seen Adam this happy since before his ex left him."

"How's Carla doing?" Drake asked.

"She's still in shock. I talked with her this morning and she's trying to come to terms with the fact that her sister is a murderer and her fiancé was an accessory to murder. I invited her here tonight but she declined. She said it was too early to get out and face people. I think it will take time for her to heal."

ACKNOWLEDGEMENTS

I would like to acknowledge and thank the staff for their hard work on the book cover and layout of *A Lethal Proposal* and the editors who pulled the story into shape.

Make sure to check out the first in this series:

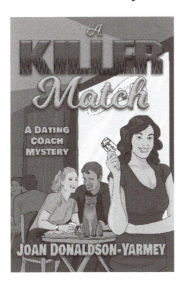

A KILLER Match

Joan Donaldson-Yarmey

Jenna Hamilton is a dating coach and the co-owner of a bookstore, with Adam Owens, in the Net Loft on Granville Island in Vancouver. When her best friend, hairdresser Hillary, is a bystander in a car crash that kills her co-worker Bruno, Jenna is there to provide emotional support. But soon, Bruno's condo is trashed, along with the salon where he used to work with Hillary.

As Jenna tries to make sense of what is happening, she makes some shocking discoveries about Bruno's life, and realizes the facade he had presented to those around him was an almost complete fabrication. Who was Bruno, really? Did someone intentionally kill him? And what are they after?

If you enjoyed this book, please consider

leaving a review where you bought it.

You may also enjoy these other Renaissance titles

ARIES

A Burning We Will Die

BETTY GUENETTE

Nurses traditionally care for bodies; they don't find murdered ones. Erin Rine, a gutsy, thirty-year-old nurse, inadvertently steps into murder when she trips over her patient's body. With her headstrong Aries personality, a black belt in taekwondo, and only fearing the unpredictable bear population in her Northern Ontario woodland districts, Erin gets caught up in the investigation with the help of her best friend, an elderly neighbour who provides astrological influences, eerily apt psychic warnings.

Burned in prior relationships, Erin is disconcerted by her attraction to the handsome investigating detective and strives to avoid a romantic entanglement despite the investigation bringing them closer.

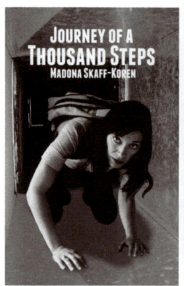
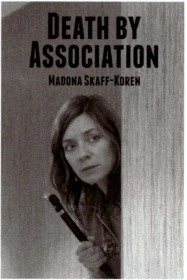

Journey of a Thousand Steps

Death by Association

Madona Skaff-Koren

Naya had the perfect life. Co-owner of a fast-growing security software company, she ran marathons in her spare time. Suddenly everything changed when she developed multiple sclerosis, and now she can barely climb a flight of stairs. Hiding at home, her computer the only contact with the outside world, she reconnects with her childhood best friend. But when her friend disappears and the police dismiss her concerns, Naya leaves the safety of her home to find her. She ignores her physical limitations to follow a convoluted trail from high tech suspects to drug dealers, all while becoming

Milton Keynes UK
Ingram Content Group UK Ltd.
UKHW021038200524
442968UK00016B/1269